'You just do[...]
she exclaime[...]

'You really can't see why I don't want your help.'

'Too damn right I can't,' he said. 'Dammit, Rachel, we're friends—'

'You keep saying that, but we're not,' she said, driven beyond endurance. 'We were lovers six years ago—'

'I thought we were both,' he said, his eyes catching and holding hers. 'Lovers and friends, and that's what I'd very much like us to be again.'

She would, too, if she thought there was any future in it, but there wasn't.

'No, David.'

'What do you want, Rachel? The moon, the stars? I'll get them for you.'

She didn't want the moon, or the stars. She wanted him to love her.

THE BABY DOCTORS

The gynaecology ward at the Belfield Infirmary,
Glasgow, is a very special place, and it employs a very
special team of people. Doctors who are all dedicated
to helping patients fulfil their dreams for a family by
helping them bring babies safely into the world.
Some of these doctors have families of their own;
some are still searching. Some of them are married
to each other; some of them are meant for each other.
But whatever their personal problems
they are all committed to giving their patients
the best chance of a child.

**THE BABY DOCTORS—
making families is their business**

Other books in *The Baby Doctors* trilogy
by Maggie Kingsley:

DOCTOR AND SON
THE SURGEON'S MARRIAGE

THE PLAYBOY
CONSULTANT

BY
MAGGIE KINGSLEY

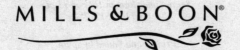

MILLS & BOON®

First published in Great Britain 2003
Harlequin Mills & Boon Limited,
Eton House, 18-24 Paradise Road, Richmond, Surrey TW9 1SR

© Maggie Kingsley 2003

ISBN 0 263 83479 4

Set in Times Roman 10½ on 11 pt.
03-1103-51772

Printed and bound in Spain
by Litografia Rosés, S.A., Barcelona

CHAPTER ONE

'BUT, Woody, I thought you'd be pleased,' Gideon Caldwell exclaimed, seeing the clear dismay on his specialist registrar's face. 'You've been saying for ages how stretched we are in Obs and Gynae, how much we need a separate infertility clinic—'

'Yes, but that doesn't mean I expected to come back from a three-month leave of absence to find one up and running, and me seconded to it,' Rachel Dunwoody protested.

The consultant sighed as he sat down behind his desk. 'The trouble is, it's *not* up and running, and that's why David needs you. He only started work officially this morning, you see, and until he can interview and appoint his own staff, he can hardly be expected to run the department on his own.'

'No, but—'

'Woody, having badgered Admin for the last three years—practically camped on their doorstep to get them to agree to this infertility clinic—we can hardly turn round and say we're not going to do anything to help it.'

He was right, they couldn't, but how to explain to Gideon that the one thing that had kept her going during the three months of her compassionate leave had been the thought that once she came back to work she'd be able to forget her troubles in her old routine, lose herself in familiar work. He'd want her to explain, and she didn't want to explain, didn't want even to think about it.

'Gideon—'

'You've always been interested in infertility work. I remember all the effort you put into that polycystic ovarian case—'

'Yes, but—'

'And helping David will mean you'll be in at the start of something big. Something that is going to make a real and lasting impact on the Belfield Infirmary. Of course, it's a challenge, but it's a golden opportunity for you, too.'

'Isn't that what con artists and time-share salesmen usually say just before they sell you a lemon?' Rachel said dryly, and Gideon laughed.

'I suppose so, but—'

'Gideon, much as I'd like to help—' like hell she would '—I don't see how I can. We're scarcely overstaffed in Obs and Gynae as it is, and if I swan off and help this new consultant—'

'David and I have come to an understanding. He's agreed that though you'll be working most of the time with him, you can come up and help me in Obs and Gynae if things get really fraught here.'

She stared at her boss open-mouthed for a moment, then gritted her teeth. 'Let me get this straight. This golden opportunity you're offering me—this wonderful challenge—consists of me not only helping to get this clinic up and running—conducting consultations, doing whatever surgery the new consultant wants—but working in Obs and Gynae *as well*?'

The consultant had the grace to look a little shamefaced. 'Something like that,' he muttered, and she shook her head at him.

'Gideon, you're not landing me with a lemon, you're dumping a whole damn orchard on me.'

'I know it won't be easy—'

'You can say that again!'

'But he has to have somebody to help him.'

'Then what about Helen?' she demanded. 'She's an SHO, and a terrific organiser. Or Tom—he's a specialist registrar like me—and he has tons more experience.'

'I agree Tom's more experienced, and you're right about Helen being a good organiser, but I don't think it would be appropriate to ask either of them to help out at the moment, do you?'

Rachel bit her lip. Of course it wouldn't. Not when the couple's daughter was still in hospital after being knocked down by a car last month. Which meant she was stuck with a job she didn't want, unless...

'Annie—what about Annie? I know the two of you just got married, and Jamie needs time to get used to you being his dad, but she's bright, keen—'

'And just a junior doctor. David needs somebody with surgical skills, and...' Faint colour appeared on Gideon's cheeks. 'Well, the thing is, she's ten weeks pregnant. I know.' He nodded ruefully as her eyebrows shot up. 'It came as a bit of a surprise to us, too. We'd planned on waiting a couple of years before giving Jamie a little brother or sister, but it must have happened on our honeymoon, so...'

She was stuck. Well and truly stuck.

'It will only be for the next two, three months, tops,' the consultant continued quickly. 'And you won't be on your own. I've said Annie can help out two days a week, doing the blood, urine and progesterone tests.'

'Big deal,' Rachel muttered under her breath, but Gideon heard her.

'Woody, you'll enjoy working with David, I know you will. His references from the Merkland Memorial are quite excellent.'

'He worked at the Merkland?' That was interesting. Interesting and surprising. The Merkland was a modern, state-of the-art hospital on the south side of Glasgow. The Belfield Infirmary dated back to Victorian times, and it showed. 'What on earth made him apply for a post here?'

'Annie says he's been wanting to concentrate solely on infertility treatment for years, so when he saw this post advertised he jumped at it.'

'Annie says?' She frowned. 'I'm sorry, maybe my lift isn't going all the way up this morning, but how would she know?'

'Because David's her brother, of course,' he said impatiently. 'Good heavens, Woody, surely you must have heard her talking about her gifted older brother?'

She hadn't, but, then, she and Annie had never been friends, merely colleagues.

So the head of this new clinic was Annie's brother and Gideon's brother-in-law. Well, that was cosy. That was dandy. That was—

Annie's brother? But if this new consultant was Annie's brother, that meant his name was David Hart.

So what? her mind protested as her heart performed an uncomfortable back flip. There had to be hundreds—if not thousands—of men in Glasgow called David. OK, so Hart might be a more unusual surname, but it couldn't be him, it simply *couldn't.*

'Gideon...' She moistened her lips and started again. 'This David Hart...'

'He's an excellent surgeon, Woody, and I think you'll learn a lot from him.'

She had a horrible suspicion she might already have.

'Gideon—'

'Speak of the devil,' the consultant beamed as the door of his room suddenly opened. 'Come in, David. Come in and meet Woody.'

Rachel spun round in her seat and her heart slid to the pit of her stomach. What was it Humphrey Bogart had said in that old black-and-white film?

'Of all the gin joints, in all the towns, in all the world, why did you have to walk into mine?'

Well, the Belfield Infirmary wasn't a gin joint, and Glasgow most certainly wasn't Casablanca, but old Humphrey sure as heck had known what he'd been talking about.

David clearly thought so, too, judging by the way he came to an abrupt halt in the doorway.

'*This* is the Woody you've been telling me about?' he exclaimed, glancing from her to Gideon, then back again. 'But this isn't Woody. This…this is Rachel.'

'You *know* one another?' Gideon said with delight. 'But that's wonderful.'

'Wonderful' wasn't the word that sprang into Rachel's mind. It was something altogether unprintable, but she pasted a stiff smile to her lips. 'Hello, David. Long time no see.'

'Six years, to be exact,' he replied. 'Six years next month.'

He remembered? That surprised her but, then, everything about David Hart always had.

'I thought you were still in Yorkshire,' she said before she could stop herself.

'I thought you were in London.'

Rachel very much doubted whether he'd actually thought about her at all, but managed to keep on smiling. 'I came back to Glasgow two years ago.'

'I've been here five years.' His lips curved into a smile every bit as false as her own. 'Small world, isn't it?'

Too small. Much too small. She could have bumped into him at any time. Met him on the underground, in a shop. Would she have left Glasgow if she'd known? No, she couldn't have left no matter how much she might have wanted to.

'David and I worked together at the Hebden in York,' she said, suddenly realising that Gideon was gazing at them both curiously. 'I was a junior doctor, he was my SHO.'

'Well, that's terrific—really terrific,' the consultant enthused. 'It's going to make everything so much easier.'

Actually, ten times worse, Rachel thought grimly, but the last two years of her life had been hell, so why should the next two months be any different?

'I've just been telling Woody that she'll be helping you

set up your new clinic,' Gideon continued. 'She's thrilled to bits.'

'So I see,' David observed dryly, and pride and self-preservation brought her chin up.

'Of course I'm pleased,' she said. 'We've been wanting our own infertility unit for years, and to be in at the beginning—helping you organise it—I couldn't be more delighted.'

And that's well and truly taken the wind out of your sails, she thought with satisfaction, only to feel her heart slip a further few centimetres when a knowing gleam appeared in his deep blue eyes. Lord, but he hadn't changed a bit. OK, so maybe he was a little heavier, a little more muscular, but he still had the same thick blond hair, the same impossibly broad shoulders, and he was still—oh, yes, dammit—he was still as handsome as ever.

But she wasn't twenty-three any more, she reminded herself as he pulled over a chair and she caught a whiff of an all too familiar aftershave. She was twenty-nine, a specialist registrar and an independent career-woman. All right, so David had unexpectedly—and that had to be the understatement of the year—come back into her life again. So what? She could handle it. She—

'Y-you're not leaving?' she stammered as Gideon walked towards his consulting room door.

'There's no point in me hanging around now I've discovered you're old friends,' he said. 'Good luck with the clinic, and if you hit any snags, just holler.'

I've already hit one, Rachel thought as the door closed behind him, and she turned to find David's eyes fixed on her. It's called what do you say to a man you last saw six years ago? A man who'd been your lover, and who knew your body as intimately as you knew his.

Well, this is a surprise?

Too feeble.

Do you still have a thing about twofer showers?

Disastrous.

Work, she told herself. Stick to work. Work is safe, neutral and uncontroversial. If we talk about work, neither of us is going to be forced to remember a time we must surely both want to forget.

'Gideon has collected all the files we have on infertile couples,' she said, indicating the stack the consultant had left on his desk. 'As you can see, there's rather a lot so I suggest we go through them one by one and make out an appointment schedule. Once word gets out that the Belfield has its own infertility clinic, I suspect we'll be inundated with requests for appointments.'

'Gideon said you'd been away on compassionate leave because your aunt died?'

She wished Gideon hadn't. She wished the consultant hadn't told him anything about her, but she nodded. 'Now, you're obviously going to need some days left free for operating—'

'That would be your Aunt Mary? The aunt who took care of you after your parents drowned in the boating accident when you were seven?'

Rachel blinked. 'You've a very good memory.'

A smile curved David's lips. A smile that didn't quite reach his eyes. 'Oh, you'd be surprised at how much I remember about you, Rachel.'

She didn't like the sound of that. She didn't like it at all, and quickly she pulled the stack of files closer to her and lifted one.

'Jennifer Norton, thirty-six in August. She's had three unsuccessful IVF treatments, but she's finally twenty-two weeks pregnant with twins. She gave us a bit of a scare in February when she started bleeding, but our main concern at the moment is her fluctuating blood pressure. Sometimes it's—'

'Gideon said your aunt died of motor neurone disease. Was that why you came back to Glasgow—to nurse her?'

Rachel stared down at the file in her hand, and watched the print blur beneath her gaze. 'I would have come back sooner if I'd known, but she said…' Tears clogged her throat and she swallowed hard. 'She said she didn't want to worry me, to be a burden to me.'

Out of the corner of her eye she thought she saw a slight movement, as though he'd half stretched out his hand to her then had changed his mind. 'When did you discover what was wrong?'

There was sympathy in his voice, and compassion, and she gripped the file tighter. 'I came up to Glasgow to visit her and found her lying on the bathroom floor. I thought she'd had a stroke—rushed her to A and E—and they told me.'

'It must have been tough.'

Tough didn't come even half-close to describing the last two years. To watch somebody she loved die slowly in front of her, knowing there was nothing she could do, had been almost unbearable. Then there'd been the funeral, and the reading of the will. Lord, but the will had been a bomb-shell and a half, and the repercussions had been worse.

'Rachel—'

She flipped open the file quickly. 'As I said, our major worry with Jennifer is her blood pressure. Sometimes it's normal, and sometimes it's way too high. She'd due in for a check-up next week…'

So she was determined to keep this purely professional, was she? David thought as she rattled through Jennifer Norton's file. Well, he could do the same, no sweat. Just because they'd been lovers six years ago, it didn't mean it should bother either of them now. Hell, they were both adult, mature people, and the past was past.

She'd changed a lot, though, he decided as he folded his arms across his chest and leant back in his seat.

The Rachel Dunwoody he'd known had been a bright, fun-loving girl who'd worn outrageously patterned sweaters, the shortest of short skirts, and her long auburn hair had tumbled about her shoulders. This Rachel Dunwoody was wearing a no-nonsense navy-blue suit, no make-up that he could see and her curls pulled back into a severe French pleat.

Her legs hadn't changed, though, he thought as his eyes drifted slowly downwards. She'd had great legs six years ago, and she still had great legs. In fact, she had terrific legs. Long, slender—

'You haven't changed, have you, David?'

His eyes shot up to hers. Ogling. There was no other word for it, he'd been ogling her legs, and from the slight smile in her light grey eyes she knew it.

'Can't blame a bloke for admiring the scenery, Rachel.' He grinned, and saw the smile in her eyes die.

'I'd be flattered if I didn't know just how much scenery you've managed to admire over the years. OK, let's move on to Rhona Scott—'

'Hey, just a minute,' he interrupted. 'What's that crack supposed to mean?'

'Oh, come on, David. Even back at the Hebden you were known as the SHO with the roving eye, and you're not asking me to believe you've changed since.'

A wash of colour swept across his cheeks. 'Rachel—'

'Rhona Scott,' she said firmly. 'Thirty-six. Her right Fallopian tube was completely blocked so Tom performed a cornual anastomosis in April, taking out the blockage and rejoining it. Tom's a good surgeon, and he thinks there's every chance she'll become pregnant without further intervention, but Rhona's desperate to try IVF. She seems to think it's some sort of quick-fix solution.'

It wasn't. The success rate for IVF was considerably lower than it was for tubal surgery, but right now David wasn't interested in Rhona Scott. Right now he was too angry with the woman sitting in front of him.

What right had she to make cheap jibes at his expense? OK, so he'd dated a lot of women, but he could honestly say he'd never promised any of them commitment. He'd always been up front, making it plain at the outset that he liked his freedom and independence, and for Rachel to imply he was some sort of serial womaniser…

And what about her? She was hardly squeaky clean. She hadn't played fair six years ago, and she wasn't playing fair now. Turning up like this out of the blue, looking all calm and in control. She should have looked guilty. She should at the very least have looked embarrassed or contrite, but she looked neither.

'Rachel—'

'I'll pencil Rhona in for an appointment next month, shall I?' she observed, reaching for her notebook. 'She's due in for her three-monthly check-up anyway—'

'Fine. Whatever you say. Look, Rachel—' He came to a halt as the consulting-room door opened and Gideon's secretary appeared. 'Something we can do for you?' he asked more tersely than he'd intended, and the secretary gave him a hard stare.

'It's a message for Woody,' she declared. 'Admin would like a word whenever it's convenient. Something about a form she needs to fill in because she's going to be temporarily working with you?'

Rachel nodded. 'I'll see to it. OK, who's next?' she continued as the secretary disappeared. 'Sable Mitchell. Rather a daft name for somebody from our neck of the woods, but I understand her mother was a fan of that American TV series.'

It wasn't half as daft a name as Woody, David thought irritably. He wondered who'd come up with the nickname. He wondered even more why she'd accepted it. Probably because it was sexless. A safely sexless name to go with her safely sexless appearance.

She hadn't been sexless six years ago. In fact, just remembering some of the things they'd done…

Work, he told himself. Concentrate on work. Work is neutral, uncontroversial, safe.

Oh, screw the work, he decided as she crossed her legs and her skirt rode up slightly to reveal a tantalising glimpse of slender thigh. What he wanted was an explanation. An explanation, followed by an apology, and he wanted it *now*.

'Why did you cut and run, Rachel?'

The file she was holding slipped from her fingers to the floor, and when she'd retrieved it she looked flustered. 'I didn't.'

'Rachel, you didn't even say goodbye,' he protested. 'I thought you were ill until I went round to your flat and your landlady told me you'd gone south, leaving no forwarding address.'

'I sent you a letter.'

'Oh, yes, your letter.' His lip curled derisively. '"Have been offered a job in London I can't refuse. Take care of yourself, Rachel".'

'It *was* a job I couldn't refuse,' she insisted. Actually, it had been a very ordinary junior doctor's post in one of the large teaching hospitals, but there was no way she was going to tell him that. 'David—'

'And was that the only reason you left?' he demanded.

Of course it wasn't, you big dope, she thought as she stared back at him. I left because I was in love with you. Had been in love with you from the very first day we met, but you didn't love me. Oh, you liked me well enough, found me fun to be with, and for you it was enough, but it wasn't for me. I wanted more—a lot more—so I ran before you broke my heart.

'David—'

'You could at least have told me where you were going. I couldn't phone you, contact you…'

'Did you want to?' The colour on his cheeks darkened and she smiled a little wryly. 'No, I didn't think so. Out of sight was well and truly out of mind, wasn't it, David?'

'Rachel—'

'Look, I'm sorry if I hurt your feelings, but I didn't think you'd be interested.'

'Not interested?' he gasped. 'Dammit, Rachel, we were *lovers*.'

'OK, so we were lovers,' she conceded, forcing herself to sound light, dismissive, 'but we were both young. You were twenty-six, I was twenty-three. We had some fun, a few laughs, then it ended.'

'But—'

'Oh, come on, David. You're not asking me to believe I was the great love of your life, and when I went south you became a hermit?'

'No, but—'

'You've dated other women since we split up, haven't you?'

'Well, yes, but—'

'And I've dated other men.' Not very successfully, she had to admit, but that had nothing—absolutely *nothing*— to do with the man sitting opposite her. 'In York we were strangers in a strange city, and when we found out we both came from Glasgow we became friends. Oh, all right, more than friends,' she acknowledged as he opened his mouth, clearly intending to protest. 'What we shared was very nice, very pleasant, but it was always going to end, wasn't it?'

'It would have been nice to have been at least told it *had* ended,' he retorted. 'Not learned it second-hand from your landlady.'

'OK, I should have told you, and I apologise,' she exclaimed. 'Happy now?'

He should have been. Common sense told him he should have been, but he wasn't. Instead he raked his fingers through his blond hair, and shook his head. 'Rachel, I don't think this is going to work—us working together again.'

She didn't think it would either, but wild horses would never have dragged the admission out of her. 'David—'

'Perhaps Gideon can suggest somebody else to help me.'

She would have cheered if he could, but there was only her, and she took a deep breath. 'David, if it doesn't bother me—'

'It doesn't?'

Did he look irritated? He certainly didn't look happy, and that stiffened her backbone. 'Of course it doesn't, and if you're going to make it a rule never to work with any woman you've made love to, you'd better open a clinic on Mars.'

She expected him to laugh, but he didn't. She thought he might at least have smiled, but instead he looked confused, and bewildered, and…piqued.

He was piqued, she realised. Piqued because she'd said she didn't care. Piqued because she'd walked out on him in the first place. He wasn't sorry, or upset, but piqued, and suddenly she knew she could do it—work with him. OK, so she still found him attractive—what normal, breathing woman wouldn't? But she was tougher now, stronger. At twenty-three she'd thought good sex meant love, but she wasn't so naïve any more. She was self-reliant and independent, and she could do it.

'Rachel—'

'I think we'd better get a move on if we intend getting through all these files this morning, don't you?' she said firmly. 'Now, where was I? Oh, yes, Sable Mitchell. We've performed the basic tests—measuring her blood progesterone and oestrogen levels—and she doesn't appear to be ovulating. Her laparoscopy also revealed she has a double uterus but I don't think that has contributed to her infertility, though I'm not an expert.'

No, but you've acquired a nice line in put-downs since we last met, he thought grimly. So it didn't bother her, him turning up out of the blue like this. It didn't bother her that they'd once been as close as any two people could have been. Well, that was just wonderful, that was really flattering.

And I'm behaving like an idiot, he thought as he

watched her pick up her pen, clearly expecting him to make some major pronouncement on Sable Mitchell's case. *Why am I letting her get to me like this? She's nothing to me now but an ex-girlfriend. In fact, if I'm going to be totally honest, I haven't thought about her in years, so why is she getting under my skin like this? And she is.*

David got quickly to his feet. 'I've had enough of files. I want to see how Maintenance are getting on with the refurbishment of my clinic.'

'But—'

'The files aren't going to sprout wings and fly.'

'No, but—'

'I'm the boss, Rachel, my decision,' he said, and without waiting for her reply he strode out of the room.

So he had a temper now, she thought as she shoved her pen and notebook back into her bag and hurried after him. *In the Hebden he'd been laid-back to the point of being almost horizontal. It would be interesting to find out what else about him had changed.*

No, it won't, her mind warned. *You've no interest in this man now, apart from what he's like to work with. He might have acquired a temper which would put the average two-year-old in the middle of a tantrum to shame, and you still mustn't be interested. It's called survival.*

But she was definitely going to wear high heels tomorrow, she decided when she caught up with him. At five feet six she wasn't exactly small, but she was going to get a serious crick in her neck—not to mention a decided inferiority complex—if she had to keep looking up to his six feet one.

'Where have they located this new clinic of yours?' she asked as she followed him out of Obs and Gynae and down the stairs.

'The Mackenzie unit on the third floor.'

She paused in mid-stride. 'The Mackenzie unit?'

'It has three consulting rooms, a staffroom, an office…'

'It's a dump, David.'

'Only because it hasn't been used for a couple of years because of staff shortages,' he protested. 'Admin are having it completely refurbished for me. In fact, it should be almost finished.'

She shook her head. 'David, the only chance you have of it being refurbished before next Christmas is if you sneak down to stores, grab a few tins of paint and do it yourself.'

'Nonsense,' he retorted, and she shrugged.

'Suit yourself, but I'll bet my next pay cheque the unit won't look any different this morning to when you last saw it.'

She was right, it didn't.

'This is ridiculous,' he fumed as he gazed round at the still sludge-green walls, the tangle of chairs piled up in a corner and the curtains hanging at a jaunty angle. 'I'm supposed to be seeing patients in here next week, and they'll never be able to relax in a place like this.'

'I'm afraid Maintenance isn't exactly what you'd call fast,' she observed, automatically reaching up to straighten one of the curtains.

'They'll be fast by the time I've spoken to them,' he said grimly, and she sighed.

'David, you can yell at them all you like, but Maintenance is in the same position as every other department in the hospital. It's underfunded, understaffed and has far too many things to do. If you want my advice, nip down to stores, swipe a few tins of paint and do it yourself.'

His jaw dropped. 'You're not seriously suggesting I paint three consulting rooms, a staffroom and an office?'

'I'll help you, and if we use emulsion it wouldn't take us long. We could do the files today, send out the appointment cards tomorrow and that would still leave us three days to paint the place and move all the desks and chairs back in.' A smile curved her lips as he gazed at her in obvious disbelief. 'What's the matter, David? Too much of a big-shot consultant now to be prepared to roll up your sleeves and get dirty?'

'Certainly not,' he retorted, 'but I've better things to do than become a decorator.'

'I'd have thought your first priority was to make this place half-decent, but…' She shrugged. 'You're the boss.'

Was there an implied jibe in that? He wasn't a hundred per cent certain, and decided to ignore it.

'I'll call Maintenance—light a fire cracker under them.'

'You could put a bomb under them and it wouldn't make any difference,' she observed, and that he couldn't ignore.

'Look, who's in charge of this unit?' he exclaimed, uncomfortably aware he was sounding unbelievably childish but quite unable to stop himself.

'You are, of course,' she said in surprise. 'I was simply making—'

'Snide comments at my expense. Well, snide comments don't achieve anything. Snide comments…' He swore under his breath as he suddenly noticed his sister Annie hovering at the unit door. 'Isn't there anywhere in this hospital where a person can hold a private conversation?' he demanded, only to bite his lip when his sister's eyebrows rose. 'I'm sorry.'

'I've obviously arrived at a bad time.'

'Of course you haven't,' Rachel interrupted smoothly. 'We're finished here, anyway.'

'No, we're not.'

'David, this place isn't going to look any better no matter how much we stare at it. You talk to your sister, and I'll get on with the files.'

'But—'

'Unless there's something else you'd like me to do?'

He could think of a couple of things, but neither of them were polite.

'Right. Fine,' he said tightly, and with a smile and a nod she was gone.

'I told you she was awful, didn't I?' Annie said, watching him kick an offending chair out of his way as he strode to the far end of the room. 'Bossy, opinionated, unfriendly—'

'No, she isn't,' he exclaimed, and saw his sister blink. What the hell was he doing, defending Rachel Dunwoody? She *was* bossy. She *was* opinionated. But she didn't used to be, he remembered. She used to be soft as butter and twice as sweet. 'She's certainly changed a lot, though.'

'Changed?' Annie repeated. 'You mean you've met her before?'

'At the Hebden in York. We dated for a while.'

His sister's mouth fell open. 'You're kidding.'

'I don't know what's so surprising about that,' he said. 'I've dated lots of girls.'

'Yes, but *Woody*? Jeez, David—'

'The Woody you know is nothing like the Rachel I knew,' he interrupted huffily, and Annie grimaced.

'She couldn't possibly be.'

'She was fun, Annie,' he insisted. 'Fun, and bright, and good company.'

His sister stared at him silently for a moment, then her eyes narrowed. 'You dumped her, didn't you? You took her out a few times, made her fall in love with you, then you dumped her, and that's why she's all bitter and twisted now.'

'Annie—'

'When you first met her she was kind to animals and small children, loved and liked by everybody, but you broke her heart, and—'

'Annie, this is not some cheap novelette, this is real life—*my* life—and I did *not* dump her. In fact, for your information…' He paused and dragged his fingers through his hair. 'She dumped me.'

'You're *kidding*.'

'Annie, if you say, ''You're kidding'', one more time…

Look, Rachel and I dated for a while, she got a job down in London, and it was over. End of story.'

'Is it?'

'Of course it is,' he protested. 'The only interest I have in Rachel Dunwoody now is how much use she's going to be to me in my clinic.'

And it *was* his only interest, he told himself when Annie gave him one of her I-don't-believe-you looks. He had absolutely no desire to resurrect the past or turn back the clock. This time around his relationship with Rachel Dunwoody was going to be strictly professional, and that was exactly the way he wanted it.

CHAPTER TWO

'YOU'VE missed a bit.'

David frowned as he leant the stepladder against the wall. 'Where?'

'Top left-hand corner of the ceiling,' Rachel replied. 'I can still see some of the old green paint shining through.'

He squinted in the direction of her gaze. 'Whose dumb idea was it to paint it buttercup yellow in the first place?'

'Yours,' she observed, levering the lid off another tin of paint. 'It will be brighter, you said. More welcoming, you said.'

'You should have told me I was an idiot.'

'Criticise the boss?' She shook her head. 'I wouldn't dare.'

'Yeah, right, and I'm Santa Claus.' He hauled the stepladder back across the room, took the tin of paint she was holding out to him and suddenly began to laugh. 'I can't believe I'm doing this.'

'It doesn't matter about the corner,' she said quickly. 'I don't suppose anyone will notice.'

'I'm not talking about the corner,' he interrupted. 'I'm talking about me. Me swiping paint from the Belfield Infirmary stores. Me sneaking a stepladder and paintbrushes up here and spending the last three days doing something Admin would most definitely say was not in my contract. Rachel, you've turned me into a criminal.'

'I haven't,' she protested. 'We only took the paint Maintenance would have used on the unit anyway. All we've done is speed things up a bit.'

He grinned. 'That's to be my defence, is it? I wasn't actually stealing, officer. I was simply speeding things up.'

23

'Admin won't give a damn about us painting the unit, or where we got the paint,' she insisted. 'They'll just be pleased it's done. And it's been worth it, hasn't it? We've only got those two skirting boards left in here to do, and once we put the desks and chairs back in and rehang the curtains—'

'You mean we're not going to steal new ones?' He looked crestfallen. 'And there was me thinking we'd be performing a moonlight raid on the nearest curtain shop.'

Rachel laughed. 'Don't tempt me.'

'Could I?'

David's eyes caught hers, dark and blue and gleaming, and her heart skipped a beat. Were they still talking about curtains? She wasn't entirely sure—had no intention of asking—so she laughed again, this time a little shakily. 'Look, are you going to redo that corner or not?'

'Slave-driver,' he grumbled.

'Realist, more like. If you want this place ready for Monday, we'd better get a move on.'

He muttered something which sounded suspiciously like 'Don't you ever relax?' as he climbed back up the step-ladder, but she ignored it.

They didn't have time to relax, not if they wanted to get the unit finished on time, but there was another far more important reason for not relaxing. Relaxing meant they started to talk, and talking, as she'd discovered since he'd come back into her life again, was a very bad idea. It resurrected memories. Memories it was far safer to forget.

'Rachel, could you pass me up a cloth?' he asked. 'I've splashed paint onto the cornice.'

Obediently she handed one up to him, only to sigh when he stretched up to remove the offending paint and she caught a tantalising glimpse of a broad bare back as his shirt came adrift from his trousers. Why did he have to look so damned good even in a pair of tatty old denims and a paint-spattered shirt? If there'd been any justice in the world, he would have become fat and bald during the last six years but, then, life, as she'd found out to her cost, was seldom fair and rarely just.

'You working here, or just watching?' he said, glancing down at her with a smile, and a rush of heat fluttered through her stomach.

Sexual starvation, she told herself firmly. These feelings I keep having are nothing more than the symptoms of a very bad case of sexual starvation.

Yeah, right, Rachel. And since when did you last bother about sex? You've always said it was vastly overrated and generally disappointing.

It had been, too, apart from the sex she'd shared with David. Now, that had been good. Actually, it had been incredible until she'd realised that good sex was all it had been.

'Rachel?'

Puzzlement had replaced the amusement in his eyes, and she managed a smile.

'I was just thinking about the appointment cards we sent out,' she lied. 'You do realise that if nobody turns up on Monday we're going to be spending the whole day staring at one another.'

'I can think of worse fates.'

She couldn't. Not if he kept teasing her like this, and smiling at her in that particular way.

So what if he does? her mind demanded. You know perfectly well that flirting comes as naturally to him as breathing. Yours is the only pulse that kicks up when he does it. Yours is the only heart that realises it would be all too easy to fall under his spell again, and you'd be an idiot if you did.

'What are we going to do with all these empty paint tins?' she asked, deliberately changing the subject. 'We can't put them out as rubbish or Admin will realise what we've been up to.'

'Whatever happened to Admin not giving a damn?' he protested.

'They won't, but that doesn't mean I think we should advertise.'

He frowned slightly, then his eyes lit up. 'I'll take them home with me—put them out with my household rubbish.'

'You're going to need some pretty hefty bags,' she pointed out, and he shrugged.

'I'll ask Annie to get me some when she brings in our lunch.'

She would, too. His sister had been terrific since they'd started painting. Ferrying them sandwiches to keep them going, warning them when anybody from Admin was about. In fact, everybody in Obs and Gynae had been great. The minute they'd discovered what she and David were doing they'd all rallied round, even offering to help in their lunch-hours.

'You know, it's strange,' she murmured as she got down on her hands and knees and began painting the skirting board. 'Until we started this I hadn't appreciated how good everyone in Obs and Gynae is. I mean, you think you know people, but suddenly you realise you don't, not really.' Silence was her only reply and she glanced over her shoulder to see David standing on the stepladder, a curiously arrested expression on his face. 'David?'

'Hmm?'

'I was just saying what a good crowd Obs and Gynae are.'

'A good crowd?' he repeated vaguely.

She sat back on her heels, exasperation plain on her face. 'Earth calling David Hart, come in, David Hart. I'm talking about Obs and Gynae—how helpful they've been.'

'Oh, absolutely.' He nodded vigorously. 'Really terrific.'

She stared at him uncertainly. 'Are you OK?'

'Fine—perfectly fine,' he replied, slapping more paint onto the ceiling, but he wasn't fine. In fact, he had a horrible suspicion he was losing his mind, and it was all the fault of the damned leggings she was wearing.

On Wednesday and Thursday she'd worn dungarees. Dungarees so baggy and shapeless even the most sex-starved of men would have had difficulty raising an interest. But today she was wearing leggings. Leggings which fitted her like a second skin. Leggings which showed her long slender legs to perfection, and outlined and hugged the cutest, roundest butt he'd seen in years.

Six years, to be exact.

Six years during which, if he'd thought about her at all, it had been with irritation and annoyance. Six years when he'd moved back to Glasgow, looked after his sister Annie when she'd got pregnant by that jerk Nick Henderson, and dated more women than he cared to remember. And yet now, just because Rachel was wearing those damned leggings...

'I wonder where Annie is with our lunch?' he said quickly.

Rachel glanced at her watch. 'It's not quite one o'clock yet. If you're hungry I could phone Annie...'

'Don't bother. I'm OK.'

But he wasn't, he thought, stifling a groan as she bent over again. Somehow—and he couldn't for the life of him think why—he'd gone from not thinking about her at all to doing nothing but remember. All the fun they'd had together, the laughter they'd shared and the personal things. The very personal things. Like the mole she had on her left breast just below her nipple. The tiny birthmark she had on her tummy just above...

He swore under his breath as all the blood in his head seemed to suddenly rush south. Hell, but he needed to start dating again. He'd been so busy over the last five months, trying to get Annie and Gideon together, then tying up all the loose ends at the Merkland before he'd left, but now he really, *really* needed to start dating again.

'Lunch up,' Annie called, pushing open the consulting-room door with her hip.

'Sis, you're a life-saver,' David declared, coming down

the stepladder with relief. 'Did you get my salami rolls with pickle and mayonnaise?'

'Yup, though how you can even bear to look at something so gross, far less eat it, is beyond me.' His sister put down the packages she was holding, and glanced round critically. 'You've missed a bit. Top left—'

'Hand corner,' he finished for her dryly. 'Everyone's a critic. How's Obs and Gynae?'

'Well, there's good news and bad news. The good news is Emma's being discharged from the children's ward tomorrow.'

'Oh, that's terrific,' Rachel exclaimed, running some water into the sink and reaching for the soap. 'I'll pop up later and tell Tom and Helen how pleased I am.'

'You will?' Annie faltered, then blushed. 'I'm sorry, I didn't mean... I meant, I'm sure they'll appreciate it.'

She didn't look sure, Rachel thought in confusion. In fact, she looked flustered, and uncomfortable, though why she should be either of these things was beyond her.

'Annie—'

'And the bad news?' David asked.

'Tom's clinic is running over time, we think one of Gideon's patients might have septicaemia, and the pregnant drug addict A and E sent up to us this morning has trashed the store cupboard looking for amphetamines.'

'Would Gideon like me to come up and help?' Rachel asked, feeling suddenly guilty. 'There's hardly any painting left in here to do, and maybe one of the porters would help David with the furniture...'

'Gideon would far rather you stayed and completed the unit,' Annie replied. 'He's as anxious as David is for it to be a success.'

He was, too. Having nagged Admin for a separate infertility unit for years, the consultant was going to be devastated if it turned out to be a turkey.

'Rachel's stressing, thinking nobody is going to turn up,' David observed, and his sister chuckled.

'Frankly, I think you'll need crush barriers. Think about it, Dr Dunwoody,' she continued when Rachel looked unconvinced. 'Wouldn't you move heaven and earth to get here if you'd been waiting two years to see an infertility expert?'

'Probably.' Rachel smiled, only for her smile to fade as she picked up her salad on rye sandwich and noticed David was frowning at her. 'What?'

'You don't eat enough.'

'I eat plenty.'

'No, you don't. You're skinnier than you were in York.'

'David, you can't possibly remember how much I weighed six years ago.' Actually he probably could, she thought grimly. He probably kept a little black book with the vital statistics of every girl he'd ever dated carefully logged into it. 'And what's it to you anyway if I've lost weight?' she demanded. 'You weren't my keeper in York, and you sure as hell aren't my keeper now, so get off my case.'

'I would if I weren't going to be your boss for the next few months,' he retorted. 'And the last thing I want is you keeling over because you're not eating enough.'

'Fine talk from somebody whose idea of healthy eating is salami rolls with pickle and mayonnaise,' she exclaimed. 'You ate rubbish in York, and you're still eating rubbish. In fact...' Oh, brilliant, Rachel, she thought as she suddenly realised Annie was glancing from her to David with keen interest. This is supposed to be a purely working relationship, remember, not a trip down memory lane. 'Would you like a coffee, Annie?' she said quickly. 'I'm just going to make some.'

'Not for me, thanks. I must get back to Obs and Gynae.' But Annie didn't leave when Rachel disappeared into the small office leading off the consulting room. Instead, she stared at her brother, wide-eyed with curiosity. 'Do you and Woody fight *all* the time?'

'We were not fighting,' he said stiffly. 'We were simply having a…a dietary discussion.'

His sister gave him an old-fashioned look. 'And do you have a lot of these dietary discussions?'

'Look, we're getting on fine. We *are*,' he insisted when Annie shook her head at him. 'Why shouldn't we be?'

'Because you and she were once…well, you know.'

'I think ''lovers'' is the word you're struggling for,' he said dryly, 'but the important word here is ''were''. What Rachel and I had—it's over, finished, in the past.'

Which sounded fine when he said it, but somehow not quite so convincing when he actually thought about it. In fact, every time he thought about it, it rankled. *He* wasn't bothered about the past—of course he wasn't—but he thought Rachel might have been, and yet if he hadn't known differently he would have sworn they'd been no more than passing acquaintances in York.

'You just be careful, OK?' his sister said, watching him.

'Of what?' he protested.

'I don't know, and that's what worries me.'

'Annie—'

'I have to go,' she declared when Rachel reappeared, carrying two mugs. 'Is there anything else you need?'

'Only some large carrier bags to put all these empty paint tins in,' her brother replied.

'And would you tell Tom and Helen I'm thrilled about their daughter?' Rachel said as Annie began walking towards the door. 'And I'll be up to see them later.'

Annie nodded, but as she left Rachel noticed she had that strange expression on her face again, the one she didn't understand.

'Is your sister all right?' she asked the minute Annie was gone. 'She seemed a bit…' Odd was what she'd been about to say, but odd hardly seemed the most tactful thing to say to a man about his sister. 'Distracted' she settled for instead.

'She's suffering really badly from morning sickness,'

David replied, biting into one of his salami rolls with rel-ish. 'Once she gets into her second trimester she'll be fine.'

'She is happy, though,' Rachel pressed. 'About the baby?'

A rueful smile creased one corner of his mouth. 'Shell-shocked would be more accurate. Gideon's over the moon.'

'I've noticed.'

His smile broadened. 'Kind of hard not to, isn't it, when he's walking around looking like he's won the Nobel prize for medicine?'

She laughed. 'A lot of first-time fathers get that look.' She shot him a curious glance. 'Ever been tempted your-self?'

'Lord, no. Oh, don't get me wrong. I love my sister's son to bits, but being a father…' He shook his head. 'It's not me.'

'I guess it would rather cramp your style,' she observed, and he met her gaze with a long, level stare.

'So you have claws now, do you?'

'Just telling it the way I see it, David.'

'And do you always tell it the way you see it nowa-days?' he asked, taking a sip of his coffee.

'I'm not a pushover any more, if that's what you mean.'

A disconcerting gleam of amusement appeared on his face. 'No wonder my poor sister's scared to death of you.'

Her mouth fell open. 'She's not.'

'Bossy, opinionated and unfriendly. And those are the only words I'd care to repeat.'

Anger flared inside her. He was making this up, she knew he was. Annie wasn't frightened of her. Why should she be? OK, so maybe she didn't suffer fools gladly, but there was no room for mistakes in medicine, and Annie knew that. David was just trying to wind her up because she'd made that crack about fatherhood, and she wasn't going to let him.

'Cat got your tongue?' he continued when she lifted her

mug and deliberately carried it to the far corner of the consulting room.

'I didn't think you were expecting an answer,' she replied, her voice ice-cold as she sat down on the floor. 'I thought you were just doing a hatchet job on my character.'

David held up his hands. 'Hey, pull in your claws, tiger. We're friends, remember?'

'Are we?'

His lips parted, then closed on whatever comment he'd been about to make. 'Perhaps we should change the subject.'

'Suits me.'

'So, did the job in London turn out to be as good as you'd expected?'

Hell, but when he'd suggested changing the subject she hadn't expected him to go back to the past. And certainly not to a part she'd lied about.

'It was interesting,' she said, deliberately vague. 'Different.'

'So, which hospit—'

'I only stayed there a year,' she continued quickly. 'Then I was offered an SHO post at the Arundel.'

'I'm impressed. No, I mean it,' he insisted as her eyebrows rose cynically. 'The Arundel has one of the best obs and gynae departments in the country.'

It did, but as he crossed the room and sat down beside her the last thing she was thinking about was the medical facilities at the Arundel. She was too busy trying not to do something really dumb and wimpy, like leaping to her feet and scurrying across to the other side of the room.

Which was crazy. OK, so he was sitting beside her, his head resting against the same wall, his long legs just inches away from hers, but he wasn't crowding her. His mind was full of medical facilities, not sex, so there was no reason for her to feel suddenly panicky, and edgy, and vulnerable.

'Why did…?' Her voice had come out ridiculously high, and she took a bite of her sandwich and started again. 'Why did you come back to Glasgow? I thought you were settled in York.'

He shrugged, then a grin tugged at the corners of his mouth. 'Maybe York just wasn't the same without you.'

'Yeah, right, David. So how long did it take you to start dating again after I left?'

'Hey.'

'A week—a fortnight?'

A dull flush of colour crept up his neck. 'I can't remember.'

'Liar.'

His colour deepened. 'And what about you? You're not telling me you've been living like a nun for the last six years.'

It occurred to Rachel that she didn't have to tell him anything, but neither did she want him to think she'd been sitting home watching TV for the last six years either.

'Of course I haven't,' she said lightly. And she hadn't. Not completely. She'd dated one of the doctors at the Arundel for four months, and then a technician from the haematology department for almost a year, and if both relationships had eventually petered out, it hadn't been because she'd still been carrying a torch for the man sitting beside her.

'And now?'

'Now?' she repeated.

'Is there a man in your life at the moment?'

There wasn't. In fact, she hadn't been out on a date for three years. After the disaster with the technician she'd decided to concentrate on her career for a while, but he'd have had to drag her over hot coals to get her to admit that.

'There is somebody,' she said, screwing up the wrapper from her sandwich and tossing it across the room. Well, the man who owned the corner fruit shop kept chatting her up, so it wasn't a complete lie.

'Does he work at the hospital?'

'I don't think that's any of your business,' she said firmly.

'You're right. It's not. So, does he?'

She stood up quickly. 'David, if all you're going to do is grill me about my private life, I'm going back to the skirting boards.'

He reached out and caught hold of her hand. 'I'm sorry. I'm just being nosy.'

'I'm glad we've got that established. Now, if you'd let go of my hand…'

'Look, about your Aunt Mary, I just wanted to say…' He rubbed the back of his neck awkwardly. 'Hell, I know words can't help, but I just wanted to say I'm very sorry.'

He was wrong. Words did help. Words, and the sympathy in his face, and the warm pressure of his fingers round hers.

'I'm sorry, too,' she said with difficulty.

'She was your last living relative, wasn't she?' he continued, only to immediately wish he hadn't when her face suddenly became shuttered.

'She had a son,' she muttered. 'My cousin Greg.'

Who didn't appear to be the flavour of the month, judging by her expression. Or perhaps he was. Perhaps he was very much the flavour, but she just didn't want to talk about him. Oddly enough, the idea annoyed him. A lot.

'Rachel—'

'We'd better get back to work.'

'Will you forget about work for a minute?' he protested.

'We can't if you want me to finish that skirting board, then help you move all the furniture back in this afternoon.'

'We've got the weekend.'

'I've things to do this weekend.'

'Hot date with Greg?' The words were out before he

could stop them, and he swore inwardly as she pulled her hand free, her expression even tighter than it had been before. 'Rachel—'

'You always did have a one-track mind, didn't you, David?'

'Now, just a minute…'

Rachel didn't give him one. She simply swung round on her heel, walked across the consulting room, and picked up her paintbrush.

Jeez, but Annie had been right. All he'd asked had been whether she had a date and she'd chewed his head off. OK, so perhaps he shouldn't have asked, but he'd been curious, and now she'd gone into major sulk mode. Well, two could play that game, he told himself. He could sulk just as much as she could.

But not half so effectively, David discovered as the afternoon wore on and she helped him move the furniture back in then hung up the curtains, without saying a word. He might be stubborn, but she took the biscuit, and he couldn't disguise his relief when Helen appeared just after four o'clock.

'If I'd known I was going to get such a welcome I'd have come down earlier,' the SHO chuckled as he strode towards her with a broad smile.

'It's a pleasure to see you any time, Helen,' he replied, and heard Rachel give a faint, derisive snort. 'Are those the carrier bags I asked for?'

'I just hope there's enough. It's not something we normally get asked for in Obs and Gynae.' The SHO glanced round admiringly. 'This looks fantastic. How on earth did you manage to get it finished so fast?'

It was easy if the person you were working with didn't talk or stop for luxuries like coffee, David thought wryly, but he didn't say that.

'How's Obs and Gynae?' he asked instead. 'Annie said it was a bit fraught this morning.'

'It's OK at the moment so Gideon would like you to

phone him if you've a minute. He thinks he might have found you a receptionist.'

'Is it one of the agency girls?' Rachel asked as soon as David had disappeared into their office, and Helen shook her head.

'It's Pam Barnes, and I do hope David takes her. She's been looking for full-time work for ages.'

'Pam Barnes?' Rachel repeated blankly, and the SHO nodded.

'You must remember her. She helped out in Obs and Gynae last year when Doris had flu. Small, brown hair, glasses?'

The description didn't ring any bells, and quickly Rachel changed the subject. 'Annie told us Emma's being discharged tomorrow. I'm so pleased for you and Tom.'

'You are?' Helen exclaimed, then flushed slightly. 'Sorry, that was a really dumb thing to say, wasn't it?'

Not dumb, but odd. In fact, almost as odd as Annie's expression had been earlier when she'd expressed her pleasure at the news.

And you're getting paranoid, she told herself. Annie's expression wasn't odd, and neither is Helen's comment. It's all in your imagination, and it's all David's fault. He's got you so wound up you don't know whether you're coming or going.

'How are you going to manage when Emma comes home?' she asked. 'She'll need physiotherapy, won't she? And with you and Tom both working…'

'My mother's coming to stay with us for a few weeks.' Helen laughed. 'I have to say Tom's holding up pretty well under the circumstances.'

'He and your mother don't get on?' Rachel said tentatively, and Helen rolled her eyes.

'That's putting it mildly, but Tom's under strict instructions to keep his tongue between his teeth for the duration.'

'Look, I could help out if you want,' Rachel suggested.

'I won't be on call in the evenings until the infertility unit is fully up and running so it would be no trouble.'

'It wouldn't?' Helen faltered, and this time there was no misunderstanding her expression. She was stunned and amazed, and Rachel's heart twisted inside her.

How had this happened? When had she become the sort of person no one would ever dream of approaching for help, a woman everybody was frightened of? OK, so she'd deliberately toughened herself up over the years, particularly when her aunt had become ill because she hadn't wanted to break down in front of her colleagues, but she hadn't thought she'd done it to the point where people thought she was uncaring and unfeeling.

Her throat closed for a second, and she took an unsteady breath. 'Helen, about Emma—'

'Mrs Barnes sounds absolutely perfect.' David beamed as he came back into the consulting room. 'Efficient and experienced, but also very sympathetic and caring, according to Gideon.'

And I don't even remember who she is, Rachel thought miserably, which proves I'm as cold and remote as my colleagues clearly think I am.

Helen and David were laughing about something, but she couldn't join in, couldn't say a word, and when the SHO had gone, David shot her an irritated glance. 'What's up with you now—got a thing about laughter or something?'

'No—oh, no!' she protested. 'I just…' She stared down at her hands for a second, then forced herself to meet his gaze. 'I'm a bitch, aren't I?'

His jaw dropped. 'What in the world put—?'

'Your sister's terrified of me, Helen looked at me as though I'd sprouted two heads when I offered to help look after her daughter, and I haven't a clue who Pam Barnes is despite the fact that she worked for us last year. What else am I if I'm not a bitch?'

'Dedicated. Focused?' He sighed as she shook her head.

'Rachel, Gideon wouldn't say you were one of the best specialist registrars he's ever worked with if you were a bitch.'

But that's my qualifications he's talking about, she thought unhappily, not me. He didn't say I was nice, or kind, or sympathetic. He said I was good at my job, and my job's not me. Or at least it shouldn't be.

'Look, why don't we celebrate finishing the unit by heading for the canteen?' David continued, watching her. 'Treat ourselves to some coffee and wickedly indulgent sticky buns.'

He felt sorry for her. He felt sorry for the woman everyone thought was a bitch, but she didn't want his pity, couldn't handle it.

Rachel reached for her bag and coat. 'Thanks, but I've things to do. I'll see you on Monday.'

'At least let me drive you home,' he protested, coming after her. 'It's 53 Mount Stewart Street, right?'

She stopped in surprise. 'How did…?'

He grinned. 'You told me your aunt's address once, and I've never forgotten it. You *are* still living in your aunt's house, aren't you?'

In a manner of speaking, she thought. 'Yes, I'm still living there.'

He shot her a curious glance but said nothing. In fact, he didn't say anything at all until he drew his car to a halt outside her house, then he glanced across at her and sighed. 'Rachel, believe me, you are *not* a bitch.'

And how would he know? 'Thanks.'

'Look—' He paused and squinted past her with a frown. 'Who's that?'

Her heart slammed against her ribcage as she followed the direction of his gaze. Her front door was open, the door she knew with absolute certainty that she'd locked this morning, and her cousin Greg was standing on the doorstep.

'It's my cousin,' she muttered.

'He lives with you?'

His voice sounded odd, slightly constricted, but she had neither the time nor the desire to enlighten him. 'I have to go.'

'But...'

'I'll see you on Monday.'

'But, Rachel—'

Rude, Rachel, her mind declared as she scrambled out of the car and raced up the steps to her house. Very rude, but civility wasn't uppermost in her mind. Finding out how her cousin had got into the house was.

'Welcome home, little Rachel.' He beamed as she pushed past him into the hallway.

'How did you get in?' she demanded. 'I locked that door this morning.'

'I still have a key. My dear departed mother forgot to ask for it back when she threw me out three years ago.'

'She didn't throw you out, Greg,' she exclaimed, dumping her bag down on the hall table and making a mental note to have every lock in the house changed tomorrow. 'She simply asked you to get a job, and when you wouldn't—'

'Have you sold the house yet?'

She gritted her teeth with exasperation. 'As I've told you dozens of times before, you're asking too much for it. Nobody is going to pay £120,000 for your mother's house.'

'It's insured for that.'

'Greg, there's a huge difference between an insurance valuation and a market valuation. The house is old. It needs a lot done to it.'

'You haven't even tried to sell it, have you?' he said. 'You just want to sit here, all cosy and comfortable, and watch me sweat. You're the one who talked my mother into changing her will, cutting me out of everything.'

'I didn't.'

'But you reckoned without Scots law, did you?' he

sneered. 'That she couldn't legally cut me out, and I was due half of the house and money.'

She wondered if she should point out yet again that she'd given him all of the little money there'd been in his mother's bank account, but what was the use? He never listened.

'A couple are coming to see the house this weekend,' she said. 'Maybe they'll put in an offer.'

He took a step towards her, and involuntarily she stepped back. He'd always been big, even when they'd been kids, but in the dimness of the hallway he suddenly looked an awful lot bigger.

'You'd better hope that they do, Rachel,' he said softly, 'because I'm running out of patience, and you know what happens when I run out of patience.'

She did. In fact, she could still remember the time he'd broken her arm when she was twelve because she wouldn't tell him where she'd hidden the stray kitten he'd been torturing.

'I…I'd like you to go now,' she said through lips gone suddenly dry, and he smiled.

'I'm going, but I want my money, and I want it soon.' He walked to the front door and opened it. 'You've a month to sell the house.'

'Greg, even if the people coming this weekend show an interest, it will take a lot longer than a month before everything's settled,' she protested. 'They'll want a surveyor's report, then they'll have to put in their offer, and—'

'Two months, then. You have until the beginning of August, and then…' He smiled again. 'I have a feeling you won't like my "and then", Rachel.'

She knew she wouldn't, but how could she sell a property that even the most enthusiastic of home decorators would have blenched at?

She couldn't, she realised, sagging back against the wall as Greg left, so what the hell was she going to do?

Tell David, her mind suggested, but she couldn't. It was her problem, not his, and she was supposed to be distancing herself from him, not inviting him back into her life.

Which meant she had to deal with it herself. She didn't know how, but somehow she had to, and then maybe the nightmare that had been her life for the last two years would be finally over.

CHAPTER THREE

'I WAS right about the crush barriers, wasn't I?' Annie declared breathlessly as she almost collided into Rachel in the doorway of the Mackenzie unit's small office. 'All those appointment cards you sent out last week, and we haven't had a single no-show all day.'

They hadn't. In fact, since they'd opened their doors at nine o'clock their waiting room had been packed, and the phone hadn't stopped ringing.

'I've never seen anything like it,' Pam Barnes exclaimed, squeezing past Rachel to answer the phone yet again. 'Good grief, anyone would think we were selling something here, instead of simply running a clinic.'

Rachel smiled, but the secretary was wrong. They weren't simply running a clinic. They were offering hope. Hope to all the nervous, anxious couples they'd seen that day that maybe—just maybe—they might one day become parents.

'Who's left in the waiting room?' she asked.

'Sable Mitchell and Jennifer Norton, but I think Mr Hart wants to see Mrs Norton.'

Rachel wasn't surprised. Jennifer was one of Gideon's success stories, and David would be anxious to keep her that way. Sable, on the other hand, was very much a newbie with a long way to go.

Quickly she reached for Sable's file, and paused. Annie was suddenly leaning back against one of their filing cabinets, and she looked anything but well.

'Annie, are you all right?' she said with concern, and the young woman pressed her fingertips to her lips with a wan smile.

42

'It's this damned morning sickness. Why does nobody ever warn you that it can hit you right out of the blue in the afternoon, and evening, too?'

'Probably because nobody would ever get pregnant if they did,' Rachel said sympathetically. 'Have you tried eating dry crackers?'

'I'm single-handedly supporting the manufacturers. Look, I'll be all right in a minute,' Annie continued as Rachel frowned. 'All I need is to sit down for a bit.'

'Would you like me to call Gideon?'

'Not on your life,' Annie exclaimed. 'He's already driving me crazy, constantly trying to wrap me up in cotton wool, and I was exactly the same when I was expecting Jamie. Well, maybe not *exactly*,' she amended, 'but today hasn't been a normal day for any of us, and we're all a bit frazzled.'

Tell me about it, Rachel thought. Even David had been uncharacteristically edgy, dashing about all over the place, trying to ensure everything was running smoothly, while she…

She still hadn't recovered from her lousy weekend, and it had been lousy. Lousy, disheartening and costly.

'Saturday call-outs are always more expensive, love,' the joiner had said after he'd drunk three cups of her coffee, taken half an hour to change the locks on the house, then handed her a bill which would have paid for a holiday in Barbados.

She'd been tempted to tell him she'd remember that if his wife was ever brought onto Obs and Gynae on a Saturday, but there'd been no point. No time either, not with the couple who'd made an appointment to view the house already on the doorstep.

Not that she'd needed to hurry him away. The couple had been very nice, very tactful, but she'd known from their expressions as they'd trooped round the house that they weren't going to buy. To be fair to them, she wouldn't have wanted to buy the house either if it hadn't been her home since she was seven, but Greg wasn't going to be pleased. Greg was going to be furious.

'I really am all right,' Annie continued, clearly misinterpreting her deepening frown. 'I just need to sit down with a glass of water.'

'We've only two patients left and David and I can handle them,' Rachel interrupted. 'Go home, Annie.'

'But—'

'Home, Annie, and that's an order,' Rachel insisted, and Annie clearly took it as one because she hunched her shoulders and walked away before Rachel could say anything else.

Oh, damn. She'd meant Annie to smile, to realise she only had her best interests at heart, but Annie obviously thought she was criticising her again. She was going to have to talk to her, to apologise for somehow always seeming to appear like the biggest bitch of all time, but not now. Not when she had Sable Mitchell waiting.

'Something wrong?'

David was standing in the doorway of the office and she shook her head. 'Everything's fine.'

'Your ears are red.'

'My ears?' she repeated in confusion, and his blue eyes danced.

'They used to go red in York, too, when you were telling fibs.'

'Rubbish,' she protested, all too aware that Pam wasn't quite as engrossed in her telephone conversation as she ought to have been.

'The fib, or York?' David grinned and, try as she may, she couldn't stop herself from smiling back.

He'd always been able to do that. Make even the dreariest day seem brighter. Perhaps it was his deep blue eyes which said, Hey, come on, you're not alone in this, I'll help you. Or maybe it was his smile. That warm, all-enveloping smile which said, Trust me, believe in me, I'll make everything all right.

Except that he didn't. Not if you were naïve enough to fall in love with him. If you fell in love with him then your troubles had only just begun.

Deliberately she picked up Sable's file. 'Give me two minutes, Pam, then send Mrs Mitchell and her husband along to my consulting room.' The receptionist nodded, but before Rachel could even move the file was suddenly and quite unceremoniously whisked out of her fingers. *'Hey!'*

'Slight change of plan,' David said smoothly. 'I'd like to sit in when you talk to Mrs Mitchell.'

'Don't trust me, huh?' Rachel said before she could stop herself, then bit her lip as his eyebrows rose. 'I'm sorry.'

'Rachel, if I didn't trust you, you wouldn't be sharpening pencils for me, far less seeing any patients. I'd just like to see how you work.'

Which was reasonable. If she'd been in his shoes she would have wanted to see how she dealt with patients too, and yet she had the strangest feeling his interest wasn't purely professional. His face might be perfectly bland, but...

'David—'

'Sable Mitchell. She's your patient with the bifurcated uterus—the one who isn't ovulating, isn't she?'

'That's right,' she murmured, and he smiled.

'Sounds like a pretty straightforward case, then.'

Sable and her husband clearly didn't think so, judging from their anxious expressions when they appeared at the consulting-room door. In fact, if they'd been wound up any tighter they'd have vibrated.

'Look, nothing awful is going to happen to you this afternoon,' Rachel said gently as soon as the couple had sat down. 'All we're going to do is discuss the options available to you.'

'Right.' Sable nodded, but she didn't look any more comfortable, and Rachel leant forward with what she hoped was her most encouraging smile.

'From the tests we've performed, it seems you're simply not ovulating. It's not as bad as it sounds,' she added, seeing Sable reach for her husband's hand, clearly anticipating the worst. 'Non-ovulation might be the cause of infertility in more than thirty per cent of all couples, but luckily it's also the easiest problem to treat.'

Donald Mitchell shifted slightly in his seat. 'But what about Sable's double uterus? Surely that must affect her ability to conceive?'

'It could certainly cause her to be slightly more at risk of a miscarriage,' Rachel conceded, 'but it's very unlikely to have stopped her from conceiving at all.'

'But—'

'Look, I know you're probably going to find this hard to believe,' Rachel continued quickly, 'but a bifurcated— or double—uterus isn't all that rare. I've actually seen two others in my medical career and I'm hardly ancient.'

Sable didn't laugh. She didn't even smile. 'Then I'm not…' She swallowed convulsively. 'I'm not deformed?'

'Of course you're not,' Rachel protested. 'What happened is the two tubes, or cornua, which should have fused together to form a single uterus before you were born remained separate, and that's why you have two uteruses.'

'It still doesn't sound normal to me.' Donald Mitchell frowned. 'What happens if Sable should get pregnant— where would the baby go?'

'It honestly isn't a big problem,' Rachel insisted. 'In the two cases I've seen, one mother carried her single baby in her left uterus, while the mother who was carrying twins had one baby in her left uterus and the other in her right. Both women needed Caesareans to give birth, of course,' Rachel continued as the Mitchells exchanged amazed glances, 'but the babies were fine.'

She was good, David thought as he watched Rachel steer the conversation back to the real reason for Sable's infertility—her non-ovulation. In fact, now he came to think of it, he'd always known she would go far even at the Hebden.

Just not all the way down to London without saying goodbye.

He gritted his teeth. Why did that still bug him so much? It was water under the bridge now, part of the past, and yet still—unaccountably—it bugged him. So did a whole lot of other things he'd forgotten about her. Like how clear and fine her skin was. How direct and lovely her large grey eyes were, and her hair... Had it always been such a rich auburn colour? It didn't look dyed but, then, neither had he remembered it being quite so glossy, or thick, or eminently touchable.

But not by him, he thought ruefully. Even if he wanted to rekindle what they'd shared in the past—and he most certainly didn't—she wasn't available. She was living with her cousin Greg.

Not that it bothered him, of course. Hell, she was a free agent, and if she wanted to live with a man who looked as though he'd been hewn from a barn door, then good luck to her. He just wished she'd told him. If she'd only told him...

'So I really think Mr Hart would be the best person to advise on that.'

Advise on what? he wondered, feeling a warm tide of colour creep up the back of his neck as he suddenly realised that three pairs of eyes were fixed expectantly on him. Well, that would teach him to let his mind wander. That would teach him to be wholly, and quite unforgivably, unprofessional.

He straightened in his seat. 'I...um...I'd be very interested to hear your thoughts on the matter, Dr Dunwoody.'

For one dreadful moment he thought Rachel was going to call him on it but, though her eyes narrowed slightly, she nodded.

'I'd recommend Clomid. The side-effects are minimal and with luck it should get Sable's pituitary gland working harder to produce more hormones which should in turn stimulate her ovaries to produce eggs.'

'My thoughts exactly,' he lied, but Donald frowned.

'These side-effects… Sable and I might want a baby but I don't want her made ill.'

'The only side-effects she's likely to experience are irregular bleeds and hot flushes,' Rachel said reassuringly, 'and as we won't be keeping her on the Clomid for very long, it shouldn't prove too debilitating.'

'I don't care what sort of side-effects I have to put up with,' Sable said, shooting her husband a butt-out-of-this look. 'But what happens if this Clomid doesn't work?'

'Then there are other drugs we can try,' David declared. 'Tamoxifen and Cyclofenil come in pill form, too, and they're often very successful in treating women who don't respond to Clomid.'

And I've got to pull myself together, he thought as Rachel went on to explain to Sable that she'd need to take one pill every day during the week preceding her period. Good grief, this isn't some stranger I'm gawping at. It's Rachel Dunwoody. A woman who was once my girlfriend. A woman I haven't thought about in years so I shouldn't be behaving like some moon-struck teenager irrespective of how fine her skin is or how auburn her hair.

'They seem like a nice couple,' he forced himself to say when the Mitchells had left.

'They are.' Rachel nodded, then met his gaze quizzically. 'OK, let's hear it.'

'Hear what?' he said in confusion, and she rolled her eyes.

'David, when I was talking to the Mitchells you never took your eyes off me for a second. Every time I looked up you were staring at me, so what did I do wrong?'

Nothing, he thought, apart from somehow managing to have become even prettier now than when he'd first met her. 'You were perfect. Straight As, in fact.'

'Yeah, right.'

'I mean it,' he insisted. 'In fact, you'd make a very good infertility specialist registrar.'

'I was hoping I made a very good obs and gynae specialist registrar,' she said lightly, and he smiled.

'You do, but you've also got the perfect manner for infertility work, and that's rare.' He clasped his hands behind his head and leant back in his seat, a thoughtful frown pleating his forehead. 'I don't suppose you'd consider changing specialities, working with me permanently?'

He had to be kidding. OK, so she'd always been interested in infertility work, but to work with him permanently? She wasn't afraid to—good grief, no—but he belonged to her past, and the last thing she wanted was for him to become a part of her present and future as well.

'I think I'll stick with obs and gynae,' she replied.

'Are you sure? Like I said, you're good, and—'

'What made you decide to switch specialities?' she interrupted, desperate to change the subject. 'I always thought obs and gynae was your first love.'

'Not women?'

'David.'

He grinned. 'OK, I'll be serious. I suppose it was constantly seeing women who wanted babies but couldn't have any. I know infertility's not a disease like cervical cancer, or a debilitating, painful condition like a prolapsed womb, but meeting these women, feeling their distress…' To her surprise a faint flush of embarrassed colour crept across his cheeks. 'I guess I just thought if I could help even some of them fulfil their dreams, my work would be worthwhile.'

Her lips curved. 'Why, David Hart, you're just an old softy at heart, aren't you?'

'Hey, less of the old,' he protested. 'I'll have you know I'm in my prime.'

He sure was, she thought, feeling her heart clutch as he stretched up towards the ceiling and she saw his shirt tighten and cling to his broad, muscular chest. In his prime, and sexy as hell.

But off limits, her heart said firmly. This man would have walked out on you if you hadn't done it first. This man wouldn't recognise the word commitment if it sat up and bit him.

But he's still sexy as hell, her body whispered, and quickly she got to her feet. 'Shouldn't you be making tracks? Jennifer Norton must be wondering what's happened to you.'

'I suppose so,' he murmured, but he didn't move, and she was the one who walked over to her filing cabinet, put Sable Mitchell's file in with the others, returned to her desk, shuffled the papers on it for a few minutes, then gave up.

'You're doing it again.'

'Doing what?'

'Staring at me.'

'I'm just sitting here.'

'No, you're not,' she protested. 'You're staring at me. Have I got a blob of ink on my cheek, or a smudge of dirt on my nose, or something?'

Should he lie, or tell her the truth? Oh, what the hell. 'I was just wondering why you always wear your hair up now. You used to wear it down in York and it was much prettier.'

She blinked, then shook her head. 'What are you up to, David?'

Good question, and he was damned if he knew the answer. 'Just making an observation.'

'No, you weren't, so knock it off.'

'Knock what off?' he asked, and she sighed.

'David, I know you find it impossible not to flirt with every woman you meet—'

'Hey—'

'But I've had my turn at being your girlfriend so go find somebody else to play with.'

He gazed at her silently for a second, then a slow smile crept across his face. 'Anyone ever tell you you're gorgeous when you're mad?'

'Oh, per-*lease*. That one's so old, it's got whiskers.'

'Yup, the old ones are always the best, aren't they? He grinned, and she walked over to her consulting-room door and opened it.

'Jennifer Norton. Twenty-three weeks pregnant with twins as a result of her fourth IVF treatment. Her appointment was for half past four, and it's now a quarter to six.'

He reached out and hit the intercom button. 'Pam, could you tell Mrs Norton to come along to Dr Dunwoody's consulting room, please?'

'*My* consulting room?' Rachel said when the intercom went dead. 'But—'

'I'd like you to sit in with me when I see her.' His smile broadened. 'You can stare at me this time if you want.'

'In your dreams,' she said, and he laughed.

'OK, but it occurs to me that as you know Jennifer considerably better than I do, you could well pick up on something I might miss.'

It made sense, but she had that odd feeling back again. The feeling he wasn't telling her the whole truth. 'David—'

'She's thirty-six, you said?'

'In August.'

'Does she have a history of high blood pressure?'

'Not that we know of, but to be fair it's highly unlikely she's ever been tested quite so often.'

'Any indications of pre-eclampsia?'

Rachel shook her head. 'Tom was worried about that, too, but her blood pressure turned out to be near normal at her last check-up.'

David drummed his fingers absently on the desk for a moment, then nodded. 'OK. Let's hope the scan reveals two healthy babies and one happy mum.'

Happy was the understatement of the year. Jennifer

beamed with relief when the monitor revealed her babies were developing as normally as any conventionally conceived twenty-three-week-old foetuses ought to be.

'Thank goodness that's over,' she exclaimed. 'I *hate* having these scans. I always think you're going to tell me there's something wrong, that there's a problem, or my babies aren't active enough.'

'If your twins were any more active, they'd be performing somersaults.' David smiled. 'Would you still rather not know what sex they are?'

'Brian and I would prefer it to be a surprise.'

'Fair enough. Now, I'd just like to check your weight and blood pressure, and that's you for another month.'

'Did Dr Dunwoody tell you I had funny blood pressure?' Jennifer asked as David handed her a towel to wipe the conductive jelly off her stomach, then helped her off the examination trolley towards the scales. 'Sometimes it's up, sometimes it's down.'

'Depending upon whether you've been limbo-dancing or not, I presume,' he said, and she laughed.

He was good, Rachel thought as she watched him, but, then, he always had been. Nothing had ever been too much trouble for his patients. It had been his personal life which had been a mess. Constantly flitting from girlfriend to girlfriend, walking away as soon as he'd sensed the relationship becoming too intense.

One of the nurses at the Hebden had said he had a commitment phobia, but her aunt had snorted when she'd told her that.

'Phobia smobia. In my day we would have said he just liked playing the field.'

He still did. All that nonsense about her hair being much prettier down than up. He surely hadn't expected her to fall for that old line. More importantly, why had he spun her the line at all?

They might have had some good times in the past. OK, all right, they'd had some terrific times, but—

'Dr Dunwoody, could you check this reading for me, please?'

David's voice was calm, but one look at his face had her hurrying across the room to him immediately.

'I don't know why I've put on so much weight since last time,' Jennifer said defensively. 'I've been following the diet sheet—honestly, I have—but the kilos just seemed to have piled on this month.'

And how, Rachel thought with dismay as she stared down at the scales, but Jennifer would have to have been eating twenty-four hours a day to have put on so much weight.

'Are your legs and ankles swollen, Jennifer?' she asked quickly.

A hint of colour appeared on the woman's cheeks. 'A little bit, but everybody's ankles swell during pregnancy. It said so in my medical book.'

'And we're the medical experts,' David declared, 'so if you could just slip off your trousers for us…'

'There's no need.'

'*Now*, Mrs Norton,' he said in a voice which even Rachel would have thought twice about arguing with, and when Jennifer reluctantly removed her trousers the reason for her unwillingness became only too horrifyingly clear. Her ankles were almost twice their normal size, and as for her thighs…

'I'll get the blood-pressure gauge,' Rachel muttered.

David nodded, but they both knew it was merely a formality. Even the most junior of doctors would have known that with such grossly swollen legs and ankles Jennifer's blood pressure was going to be sky-high.

'Jennifer, I'm afraid you have pre-eclampsia,' David declared after Rachel had removed the blood-pressure cuff and helped Jennifer back on with her trousers. 'I know that sounds scary,' he continued quickly as Jennifer gasped, 'but it's only dangerous if it develops into full-blown eclampsia. I'll start you on a course of injections—'

'No.' Jennifer's face was white, but determined. 'I'm not taking any drugs. They get into your blood stream, into your babies—'

'What I want to give you isn't a drug,' David interrupted. 'It's magnesium sulphate, a compound very similar to Epsom salts.'

'I don't care what it's similar to, I'm not taking anything that might harm my babies.'

Rachel pulled a seat over to Jennifer, and sat down beside her. 'Jennifer, eclampsia is very serious. It can cause convulsions, and brain damage, and if Mr Hart says these injections won't harm your babies, they won't.'

Tears filled Jennifer's eyes, and she scrabbled quickly in her pocket for a handkerchief. 'I wish my husband was with me. He'd know what to do.'

'He'd say you should have the injections,' David said firmly. 'If you were my wife I'd insist on you having them. Four injections, Jennifer. Just one a month until your babies are born, and your chances of developing full-blown eclampsia will be halved. Pretty good odds, don't you think?'

He was giving Jennifer one of his trust-me-I-can-help-you smiles, and Rachel crossed her fingers behind her back and prayed the woman would agree. They couldn't force her to have the treatment, but the consequences to her and her unborn babies if she refused didn't bear thinking about.

'You really think it's for the best?' Jennifer said eventually.

'I do,' David replied, and after what felt like an eternity Jennifer finally nodded.

'I thought she was going to refuse,' Rachel confessed, after Jennifer had left with firm instructions to return in a month's time for her next injection and even firmer instructions to come back immediately should the swelling become worse.

'It was close,' David admitted. 'Too damn close.'

'Will she be all right?'

'Do you want an honest answer or an optimistic one?'

'An honest one,' Rachel replied, and he sighed.

'All we can do is hope that with the help of the magnesium sulphate injections she'll be one of the fifty per cent of women who don't develop eclampsia.'

'Not very scientific—just hoping, I mean,' she said, and he smiled ruefully.

'A lot of medicine isn't.'

He was right, but she wished he wasn't. She wished even more that they could wave a magic wand and prevent every woman in the world from ever developing eclampsia, and he must have read her mind because he closed Jennifer's file and got to his feet.

'Look, why don't I take you out to dinner tonight? It would cheer us both up, and be a thank you for all your hard work over the past week.'

For a second she was tempted. Going out to dinner sounded a lot better than simply going home and reheating whatever she could find in the fridge, but suddenly she was tired. Tired and a little depressed.

'Thanks for the offer, but I don't think I'd be very good company tonight.'

'We could just sit together in silence and eat.'

Rachel shook her head. 'Perhaps some other night.'

'How about if I promise not to try to flirt with you again?'

It had never occurred to her that he might, but he clearly thought that was the reason for her refusal, and a spurt of anger welled inside her.

'David, you could flirt until you were blue in the face and it wouldn't get you anywhere.'

'Sure about that, are you?'

'Cast-iron, one hundred per cent sure,' she retorted, and one corner of his mouth twitched.

'Feisty little thing now, aren't you?'

She reached for her handbag. 'I prefer to say I've grown up.'

His eyebrows snapped together. 'Meaning I haven't?'

She did, but she was too tired for an argument. 'David, it's been a long day, so let's just forget it, OK?'

She thought he was going to argue with her—he looked as though he'd very much like to—but he nodded.

'Did you enjoy today?' he asked, clearly deciding it would be safer to change the subject. 'I mean, did you find it interesting?'

She had. In fact, she'd been amazed at how very stimulating she'd found it. Stretching, too, when her speciality wasn't infertility treatment, but she had enjoyed it.

'Do you think we'll be as busy tomorrow?' she asked as she led the way out of her consulting room.

'Frankly, I can't see a time when we *won't* be busy,' he replied. 'Not with the current shortage of infertility clinics.'

He looked tired, too, she realised. Tired, and something else she couldn't quite put her finger on. 'I think you should go home—put your feet up,' she said.

'I fully intend to,' he said, only to groan when Pam suddenly appeared with a thick sheaf of papers and a determined look. 'Correction. Make that I *intended* to.'

'These will only take you a few minutes to read and sign, Mr Hart,' the receptionist said apologetically. 'Ten at the most.'

'Yeah, right,' David said ruefully, and with a wave of sympathy Rachel made good her escape.

Exhilarating though the day had been, she'd had enough. It was time to go home, but not immediately, she realised when she went into the staffroom and found Annie still there.

'I thought I told you to go home,' she protested as Annie scrambled awkwardly to her feet.

'I was just going, Dr Dunwoody—honestly I was. I'll be out of your way in a minute. I just need— Oh, damn,' she gasped as she reached for her coat and pulled the coat-

and hat-stand over in the process. 'I'm sorry—so sorry. I'll pick up everything.'

'I'll do it.'

'It won't take me a minute.'

'Annie, I said *I'll* do it,' Rachel said more sharply than she'd intended, only to groan inwardly when Annie flinched. Lord, but David had been right. His sister was terrified of her, and it was wrong, wrong. Quickly she retrieved the coats, hung them up again, straightened her shoulders and took a deep breath. 'Look, I owe you an apology, don't I?'

'You didn't knock over the coat-stand—'

'I'm not talking about the coat-stand,' Rachel interrupted. 'I'm talking about the way I've been treating you ever since you joined the staff. The way I seem to have been treating all the staff. I…I've been a bitch, haven't I?'

Annie's jaw dropped. 'You haven't.'

'Your brother told me you were scared to death of me.'

'He did *what*?' Annie spluttered. 'He had no right—'

'I'm glad he did. I hadn't realised I was being so horrible. All I can say in my own defence—and it isn't much of a defence—is that I didn't do it deliberately. Annie…' She swallowed hard, and forced herself to meet the young woman's startled gaze. 'Can you possibly forgive me, let me start again and perhaps become your friend instead of an ogre? I'd like that very much, if…if you'd let me.'

Annie looked stunned, and Rachel held her breath, hoping she would agree, wondering what on earth she was going to do if she didn't. To her overwhelming relief Annie nodded slowly and said, 'I think I'd like that, too, Dr Dunwoody.'

'It's Rachel, or it's Woody,' Rachel said firmly. 'I don't care which you use just so long as you don't yell, "Hey, you", after me.'

Annie laughed a little nervously. 'OK…Rachel.'

'OK, what?'

Both women whirled round guiltily, and it was Annie who recovered first. 'Private conversation, David.'

'Sound intriguing,' he commented, his blue eyes sparkling. 'What's it about?'

'Nothing you need to know,' his sister declared. 'I'm for home. How about you, Rachel?'

'Sounds good to me,' she agreed, throwing Annie a grateful look as she pulled on her coat. 'Are you walking, or—?'

'There's a phone call for you, Dr Dunwoody,' Pam said, appearing behind David without warning, and Rachel groaned.

'Can't it wait until tomorrow? I'm really bushed.'

'He said to tell you it was important, and his name was Greg. In fact, he made me repeat his name twice over,' the receptionist continued with obvious disgust, 'like you were stupid or something.'

Rachel didn't look stupid, David thought as he watched all the colour drain from her face. She looked suddenly sick. Very sick.

'Are you all right?' he said, starting towards her with alarm.

'I'm fine—fine,' she muttered.

'No, you're not. Sit down, put your head between your knees. Pam, tell this Greg person to call back tomorrow.'

'*No!*' Rachel exclaimed, then flushed when both David and the receptionist looked at her in surprise. 'I'll take the call in my room.'

She was gone before David could stop her, and a deep frown creased his forehead when the receptionist hurried off to transfer the call.

'I wonder what that was all about,' he murmured as his sister buttoned up her jacket and reached for her bag. 'I thought she was going to faint just then.'

'She certainly looked a little white.'

'A *little*?'

'OK, a lot,' Annie conceded, 'but maybe it's her time

of the month. Maybe she's just remembered an important appointment she'd made. David, I'm really tired, and if you're finished for the day I'd really appreciate a lift home.'

'Her cousin's name is Greg,' he continued doggedly, 'and she lives with him. As in *lives* with him, Annie.'

'So?'

'So why should she look like a ghost just because her boyfriend's called?'

His sister walked purposefully towards the door. 'Perhaps it was some other Greg on the phone. And even if it was her boyfriend,' she continued when he tried to interrupt, 'Rachel's private life is none of your business.'

'Of course it's my business,' he protested. 'We're friends.'

'Not what you'd call close friends considering you haven't seen or spoken to her in six years.'

'Oh, very smart, very clever, Annie,' he said tartly. 'Look, I'm worried about her. If she has boyfriend trouble—'

'If Rachel has boyfriend trouble, or if that was her plumber on the phone, or her long-lost transvestite brother, it would still be none of your business, David, and I'd like to go home, please.'

Not her transvestite brother, David thought as he reluctantly followed Annie out of the staffroom. Her cousin. Her live-in lover who apparently frightened the living daylights out of her.

But why in the world would she live with a man who frightened her? It didn't make any sense, unless…

His jaw clenched. There'd been a nurse at the Merkland who'd lived with a man who'd regularly beaten her up, and it had only been when she'd been hospitalised for the third time that they'd been able to get her to listen to reason. If this Greg was abusing Rachel…

Unconsciously David shook his head. Annie could say whatever she liked, but Rachel Dunwoody was very much his business and he wasn't going to rest until he found out exactly what was going on.

CHAPTER FOUR

'BP 120 OVER 80, temp normal, heart rate normal,' Barry announced from behind his array of anaesthesia equipment. 'Mrs Grant's well and truly under, David, so you can start the fimbrioplasty whenever you want.'

David glanced across at Rachel. 'Ready?'

'Whenever you are.'

'Sharon?'

'A-OK, Mr Hart,' the theatre sister replied, and David leant forward and made a quick, neat incision into Christine Grant's abdomen just above her pubic bone.

'I see Liz Baker's on the prowl again,' Barry commented as he adjusted the dials on his monitors. 'I noticed her coming out of Haematology, clutching her little red bag, and we all know what that means.'

Rachel and the theatre sister groaned in unison, and David glanced across at them quizzically. 'I'm afraid you've lost me. What's the significance of Sister Baker's little red bag?'

'She's trying to sell tickets for the July ball,' Rachel explained. 'You see, the hospital committee organises three balls a year to raise money for the special care baby unit,' she continued as David looked even more confused. 'One on St Valentine's Day, one at the beginning of July and the other at Christmas. Liz's little red bag means the July ball's on the horizon.'

A slight frown appeared between David's eyebrows as he made a second smaller incision into Mrs Grant's abdomen. 'Call me dense if you like, but why should an occasion which aims to raise money for such a worthy cause be greeted by such gloom?'

'Because all the events are the same,' Barry declared before Rachel could reply. 'BP a little raised, heart rate and pulse fine. The committee always books the function room at the Grosvenor Hotel, we always have a finger buffet—'

'And as most of the committee are old crocks, the Blue Lagooners always supply the music,' Sharon chipped in. 'It's boring.'

Annie hadn't found the St Valentine's Ball boring, David remembered as he gently slid the end of the tiny microscope into the second incision. In fact, it had been that dance which had kick-started her romance with Gideon. The dance and his idea to take Jamie home with him for the night, he thought with a grin.

'Didn't Liz say after the St Valentine's Day ball that the committee was thinking of making the July one fancy-dress?' Rachel asked, stepping to one side to let Sharon bring the trolley of tiny instruments closer.

'But that just means those cheapskates in Ophthalmology will put on their white coats and turn up as doctors,' the theatre sister protested.

'Or as Adam, sporting home-made fig leaves.' Barry grinned, and Sharon and Rachel chuckled, but David didn't.

He was too busy trying to banish the disturbing image which had popped into his mind. The image of Rachel turning up at the ball dressed as Eve. Not that he believed for one minute that she would. More was the pity. She'd probably play it safe and come as a cowgirl, or a milkmaid, though it would be a crime to cover up her glossy auburn curls with a cap.

'David?'

Rachel's eyes were on him, curious, questioning, and he flushed beneath his surgical mask. Lord, but it was bad enough not being able to forget the past, but if he was going to start fantasising about the present as well...

Quickly he sat down on the stool Sharon had placed

beside the operating tables, lined up the lenses of the tiny microscope and stared down them.

'How does it look?' Rachel asked.

'Exactly as Gideon thought,' he replied. 'The Fallopian tube is badly scarred at its outer end, but it isn't completely blocked.'

'So you can reconstruct the fimbria?'

'It would actually have been easier if the tube had been completely blocked but, yes, I can do it. Want to take a look yourself?'

She nodded, but as she took his place at the microscope his jaw tightened as his eyes fell on the slender curve of her neck and its pale, silky skin.

How could any man hit her? How could she stay with somebody who did? It made his blood boil just thinking about. Of course he knew it happened. Bright, attractive women who stayed in destructive relationships, telling themselves that their tormentor loved them, that they must somehow have provoked the attack, but for it to be happening to Rachel…

He had to get her to talk about the situation. He'd tried his best over the past fortnight, but every time he'd mentioned Greg's name she'd changed the subject. Somehow he had to get her to admit that she was in an abusive relationship, but how?

'Why on earth is the damage so bad?' Rachel murmured as she gazed down the microscope. 'I could understand it if she'd never had a baby, but she has a son aged eight.'

'Who probably inadvertently caused the damage. Sometimes when a woman gives birth she catches an infection which spreads to her Fallopian tubes,' he explained as she glanced up at him in surprise. 'It doesn't happen often, but it does happen.'

'Are you going to use a laser or scissors to remove all the adhesions from her tubes before you do the reconstructive work?' she asked as she slid off the stool.

'Scissors. I know there's a lot of hype surrounding

lasers, but to my mind nothing beats the human hand and eye.'

'Especially for removing bands of fibroids from around a Fallopian tube.' She nodded, and Barry chuckled.

'I don't know why you're bothering to advertise for a specialist registrar, David. You've got the perfect one standing right beside you.'

A deep flush of uncomfortable colour spread across Rachel's cheeks—colour that even her surgical mask couldn't hide—and David said smoothly, 'I'm afraid she's not interested.'

'Perhaps you should try changing your aftershave,' Sharon suggested, and they all laughed—even Rachel, he noticed, which was good to hear.

He hadn't heard much laughter from her during the past two weeks. To be fair, the hours they were working scarcely left much time for laughter, but those dark shadows under her eyes suggested she wasn't sleeping properly. She probably wasn't, he thought grimly. Not with Greg waiting at home for her. Waiting to hold her, to touch her, to force himself upon her, whether she wanted to make love or not.

'Let's get to work,' he said more abruptly than he'd intended, which wasn't fair when he'd been the one holding up the proceedings by asking all those questions about the July ball, but right now he didn't feel fair. Right now, he felt frustrated and helpless, and he didn't like the feeling one bit.

It was a long and painstaking operation, sore on the back and the eyes. Removing all the adhesions and every scrap of fibrous material surrounding Christine Grant's Fallopian tubes with the tiniest of scissors was hard enough, but reconstructing the delicately fronded tissue at the end of each tube required absolute concentration. Nothing short of perfection would do or the fronded tissue would have no hope of catching, and hopefully retaining, a fertilised egg.

'Would you like me to finish off for you?' Rachel asked when David eventually straightened up and rotated his shoulders. 'Suture the incisions?'

'That would be great, thanks. Irrigate the peritoneal cavity first with Ringer's lactate solution,' he continued as she took his place at the operating table. 'We have to make sure we've removed all traces of— *No, don't touch!*' She jumped as though he'd lit a fire cracker under her, and he smiled a little ruefully. 'I'm sorry, I didn't mean to yell, but you mustn't touch any of the tissue, not even with the tip of your latex gloves. It could cause new adhesions to grow.'

'I'm the one who should be apologising,' she mumbled. 'It was stupid of me— I should have thought…'

'I should have told you to use the glass rods if you needed to lift any tissue,' he said gently. 'The trouble is, I keep forgetting infertility's not your speciality.'

'I don't,' she muttered, and he glanced across at her sharply.

Did she mean she felt inadequate when faced with the work? Surely not. OK, so she'd almost made a mistake, but this was her first fimbrioplasty, and everything else he'd seen her tackle had been excellent.

'Do you want dissolvable stitches,' she continued, 'or—?'

'Dissolvable. They're easier to remove, and leave less of a scar.'

She nodded, but as she reached out and picked up one of the needles he frowned slightly.

Could she have meant she found his presence unsettling? If she did she was certainly hiding it well. In fact, there were times when she seemed so indifferent to his presence that he wanted to shake her.

I could make her notice me, he thought. I did it six years ago, and I could do it again.

Dumb, his mind whispered. Dumb idea. The past is past, and you don't want to recreate it, but…

He stared at her bent head, at the long slender arch of her neck and the tantalising curves of her body which even her shapeless theatre scrubs couldn't quite disguise.

When had she become so attractive? She'd always been a pretty girl but now, with her hair tugged tightly back into that irritating French pleat and her boring sensible clothes, she was somehow so much more attractive. Which made no sense. But, then, nothing seemed to have made sense since he'd met her again.

'How good are Christine's chances of conceiving now she's had the fimbrioplasty?' Rachel asked when the operation was over, and they were in the scrub room.

'No more than forty-five per cent, I'm afraid.'

'But if she hadn't had the surgery, her chances of conceiving would have been nil,' she pointed out, and he sighed.

'True, but tubal surgery is major surgery, and she's just put herself through a big operation, with all its accompanying psychological stress, on the strength of a forty-five per cent hope.'

Concern darkened her eyes as she pulled off her theatre cap, sending a couple of hair pins pinging to the floor in the process. 'Are you saying you wouldn't have recommended this operation if Gideon hadn't already agreed to it before you saw her?'

'There's pros and cons on both sides,' he declared, forcing himself to concentrate on her question rather than on the longing he suddenly felt to pull out a couple more of her hair pins and send her hair tumbling down to her shoulders as it had been back at the Hebden. 'But on balance I'd say Gideon was probably right.'

'Whether you think Gideon was right or not, what you did was pretty impressive surgery,' she observed, and he shrugged dismissively.

'You could do it, too, once you'd had enough surgical practice. You've got good hands, like me.' To his surprise a faint tinge of colour appeared on her cheeks. Colour that instinct told him had nothing to do with pleasure at his observation. 'Rachel—'

'You don't need me for the uterine polyps removal or the ovarian wedge resection, do you?'

'No, but—'

'I'll wait with Christine until Barry brings her round, then go back to the unit and make a start on the appointment schedule for the next four weeks.'

'Rachel…'

The sound of the scrub-room door clattering shut was his only reply, and he frowned as he dragged off his theatre top and binned it. He'd meant his observation to be a compliment about her surgical skills, and she'd obviously taken it to mean something else, but what?

He was still racking his brains when he'd completed his morning list, and he was no further forward when he strode into the Mackenzie unit and straight into Liz Baker.

'Mr Hart, the very person I'm looking for.' She beamed. 'I was wondering if I could interest you in a ticket to our annual July ball? It's a week on Saturday at the Grosvenor Hotel, and at £40 a ticket it's excellent value for money.'

'It's to be a fancy-dress affair this year, isn't it?' he said as he lead the way into the staffroom and switched on the kettle.

'Actually, a Famous Figures from History ball.'

'I'm afraid you'll still get some of the staff donning white coats and pretending to be Louis Pasteur or Alexander Fleming.' He grinned, and the sister frowned.

'Come again?'

'It doesn't matter.' He reached for the jar of coffee. 'Does Dr Dunwoody normally attend these dances?'

Liz shook her head. 'Not usually, no. She says dances aren't her thing, and usually just gives us a donation instead.'

'Does she now?' David murmured. He stared pensively at the jar of coffee for a moment, then his lips curved. 'Well, I think you'll find she'll attend this one.'

'She will?' The sister looked confused, then rallied. 'Actually, while we're on the subject of the ball, the committee was hoping you might do them a favour. It's nothing mega,' she added hurriedly as David's eyebrows rose, 'but people have been becoming a little bored with our dances lately so we thought we might make it different this time.'

'Isn't making it a Famous People from History ball different enough?' he asked, lifting two mugs from the shelf and holding one out to her questioningly.

She shook her head. 'No coffee for me, thanks. I suppose it is, but we thought it might be even more fun if we put all the tickets sold to the unmarried members of staff into two hats. One for the men, and one for the women, and then—'

'Get somebody to draw a ticket from each hat, and those people are partners for the evening,' David declared, already one step ahead of her. 'That would certainly make it…interesting. Who's going to make the draw?'

'We were hoping you would,' Liz said in a rush. 'You see, you're the newest member of staff,' she continued as he gazed at her in surprise, 'and if you did it nobody could possibly accuse you of rigging the results.'

He spooned some coffee into a mug, his expression thoughtful. 'No, they couldn't, could they?'

'So…will you do it?'

For a moment he said nothing, then a smile began to play around his lips. 'On two conditions.'

'As long as the conditions aren't too over the top, you've got them,' Liz said with obvious relief.

'I don't want to buy a ticket until you've asked Rachel if she wants one.'

She looked puzzled, but nodded. 'OK, and your second condition?'

'When she gives you her ticket to put in the draw, I want you to crease the corner of it so I'll know which ticket is hers.'

Liz's mouth fell open. 'No—no way! Look, I know

Woody can be a bit of a pain at times, but I can't—and won't—let you fix her up with one of the sleaze-balls in Ophthalmology.'

'I thought they were cheapskates.'

'They're both. Mr Hart—'

'Liz, I'm not going to fix her up with a sleaze-ball unless you consider me one.'

If Liz had looked aghast before, she now looked completely stunned. 'You want to rig the draw so you can go to the ball with *Woody*? Are you—?'

'If you're about to say, "Are you kidding", I'd far rather you didn't,' he said dryly. 'So, have we a deal or not?'

The sister chewed her lip for a minute, then nodded reluctantly. 'I think you're out of your mind, but on your own head be it. Where is Woody?'

He glanced at his watch. 'She'll be busy in her consulting room at the moment, but we usually manage to squeeze in a coffee-break at three o'clock, so if you come to the staffroom in half an hour, you should be able to catch her then.'

And after the coffee-break he'd take a quick trip down to the psychiatry department, he decided ruefully as Liz left, and tell them what he'd just done. With luck they might be able to explain the crazy, irrational plan which had suddenly occurred to him because he sure as hell couldn't.

'Dr Dunwoody, the appointment schedule you've worked out for the next four weeks is madness,' Pam protested. 'I know people are desperate to have appointments, but you've given yourselves no leeway at all. What if some emergency crops up, or if you or Mr Hart should fall ill?'

'We'll just have to hope we don't, and my name's Rachel or Woody, Pam. I keep telling you that.'

The receptionist coloured. 'I know, and I'm sorry. I just find it really hard to call you Rachel.'

So did everybody else at the Belfield, Rachel thought with a deep sigh, but she was going to keep on correcting them no matter how long it took.

'Pam—'

'Won't you please reconsider your schedule? Nobody should be working eleven hours a day, six days a week. What about your health, your social lives?'

'We'll survive,' Rachel said firmly, but when the receptionist had gone she sat down at her desk with a rueful smile.

What social life? David might have one to lose, but she… When she left the Belfield tonight she'd go home, heat something up in the microwave, watch TV, then go to bed.

Things will be different when David appoints his own staff, her mind whispered as she stared at the calendar on her wall with its picture of exotic palm trees and a white sandy beach sloping down into an azure blue sea. Pam had put advertisements in all the journals, there'd already been quite a few replies, and once David had chosen who he wanted, she could go back to Obs and Gynae and…

Go home every night from the Belfield, heat up something in the microwave, watch TV and go to bed.

'Maybe I should just buy a cat or a canary, and be done with it,' she muttered, only to swing round in her seat, red-cheeked, when she heard a discreet cough behind her. 'Annie, I didn't hear—'

'I did knock, but you were obviously miles away,' she said uncomfortably. 'Are you OK?'

No, she wasn't. 'I'm fine, thanks. What can I do for you?'

'Obs and Gynae need to know how long we're going to require bed space for the ops David performed this morning.'

'Mrs Grant might be fit enough to be discharged in five days, but we'd better say a week to be on the safe side.'

'You'll want her to have both antibiotics and steroids?' Annie said, making a note on her clipboard.

'For sure. After all the time and effort David put into reconstructing her fimbria, the last thing he'll want is her developing an infection.'

'I've never seen him operate,' Annie said. 'What's he like?'

'Brilliant,' Rachel answered, and he was. She'd watched Tom and Gideon operate many times, and though neither of them were slouches in the operating theatre, neither of them possessed David's quick, delicate hands. Hands that weren't just quick and delicate when he was operating, she remembered, but equally skilled when he was making love. In fact, she'd never forget that day when they'd driven out to the Yorkshire dales and he'd drawn her down into the grass, and—

'And the ovarian wedge resection?'

Annie's pen was poised expectantly over her clipboard, and Rachel groaned inwardly. Wool-gathering. She'd been wool-gathering about something that had happened years ago, and it wasn't just stupid, and pointless, it was also deeply unprofessional.

'The ovarian wedge resection?' she repeated with a casualness she was very far from feeling.

'And the uterine polyps.' Annie nodded. 'How long do you think they'll require beds in Obs and Gynae?'

'Two days tops for both of them,' Rachel said, opening her desk drawer and taking out her appointment book.

'Obs and Gynae are going to be relieved,' Annie commented, and Rachel sighed.

'What we really need is our own ward, but I can't see it happening in the near future.'

'That's what I keep telling David. I told him he'll just have to be patient, but you know what men are like.'

Not really, Rachel thought wistfully, and definitely not a man like David Hart. She'd never been able to figure out what made him tick.

'How's your morning sickness?' she asked, deliberately dragging her mind back to the present.

'A little better.'

Yeah, right, Rachel thought, staring at her critically. And I'm the sugar plum fairy.

'Look, Annie,' she began hesitantly, 'I don't want you to think I'm siding with Gideon or anything, but I think you could be doing too much.'

'He's been talking to you, hasn't he?'

'No, he hasn't.'

'Rachel, it's all very well for Gideon to say I should give up work,' Annie flared, 'but what would I do if I did? Sit around for the next six months, watching my bump grow? It would drive me mad.'

'It might not.'

'It would,' Annie insisted. 'No woman in her right mind would want to be stuck at home all day, knowing her husband was going to be phoning her every hour on the hour to ask how she was feeling.'

I would, Rachel thought. I'd love to have somebody care for me so much that all he wanted was to cosset and protect me. I'd love to have a baby created from that love growing inside me, but it's never going to happen. Not to me. Oh, I suppose I could go to a sperm bank, have a baby that way, but I want the whole package. A partner, a baby, a family, and it isn't going to happen.

'Rachel, I'm sorry,' Annie mumbled, her voice suddenly small. 'That was an incredibly tactless thing for me to say. I don't know your circumstances—whether you're single by choice, or childless by choice—'

'My aunt used to say I was an unclaimed blessing,' Rachel interrupted with a slightly crooked smile. 'Personally, I think she was looking at me with rather rose-tinted glasses, but I do know one thing. I'd rather stay single than settle for anything less than what you and Gideon share.'

Annie met her eyes briefly, then stared down at her clipboard. 'Rachel, I know this is none of my business, but you and David—'

'Water under the bridge, ancient history,' Rachel said briskly. 'Your brother's great fun, Annie, but he doesn't love me. Never did.'

'I don't think David knows *what* he wants, but—'

'Ah, the very person I'm looking for,' David smiled as he came into the consulting room. 'Admin's been on the phone for you, Annie. Something about requisition forms you were supposed to send down to them this morning?'

His sister clapped her hand over her mouth in dismay. 'Oh, hell's bells. I did them yesterday, then completely forgot all about them.'

She shot out of the room without a backward glance, and David chuckled and shook his head. 'I wonder why pregnancy always seems to turn even the most intelligent of women's brains to mush?'

Rachel shut her desk drawer with a bang. 'Considering the amount of hours your sister's working, not to mention having a young child to take care of, plus a husband to feed, I think she's doing wonderfully to even remember her own name.'

'Hey, I was just making an observation.'

'The kind of lame-brained observation only a single man with no responsibilities or understanding would make.'

He glanced at the door, then at her. 'Maybe I should leave and come back in again?'

'Maybe you should just leave, period.'

He leant back against the doorframe and sighed. 'Go find Annie and tell her about the forms she's forgotten. Then ask Rachel if she'd like a cup of coffee. Two apparently simple tasks and yet I seem to have screwed them both up.'

'You sure have,' she replied.

'Look, could you cut me some slack here, Rachel?' he protested. 'I'm sorry, OK? I'll even apologise to my sister if you want, but right now I'm gasping for a coffee and something to eat.'

So was she. 'Nobody's stopping you from doing either.'

'Pam brought in two chocolate éclairs and a strawberry tart for our coffee-break.'

Her stomach rumbled in anticipation. 'I'm not that cheaply bought.'

'I never imagined you were,' he said as she walked past him into the corridor.

'But the strawberry tart's mine.'

'Thought that, too.'

Rachel could hear the grin in his voice and ignored it. 'Annie's arranged everything with Obs and Gynae for the patients you operated on this morning.'

'No problems?'

'Not if the time scale I've given them doesn't alter.'

David shook his head impatiently as he followed her into the staffroom. 'All this begging and pleading for bed space. It's crazy. What's going to happen when I'm operating three days a week instead of just one?'

The staffroom phone began to ring and as David went to answer it Rachel zeroed in on the strawberry tart. 'Maybe that's Admin,' she observed, 'calling to tell you they're going to build you a brand new state-of-the-art unit with its own ward. And not just a ward, but your own operating theatre, a lab, a—'

'It's Greg.'

Her heart lurched sickeningly against her rib cage. Oh, damnation, but she didn't need this, not right now, and it was all her own fault. She should have answered the messages he'd been leaving on her answering-machine at home instead of simply erasing them, hoping he'd go away, disappear.

'He says he needs to talk to you,' David continued. 'Do you want to take the call?'

She put down the strawberry tart, her appetite gone. 'No.'

He stared at her for a second, then turned back to the phone.

Stupid, Rachel, stupid, she told herself. For the last two weeks David's been asking you questions about Greg—odd questions, personal questions—and now he's just going to want to know more, and what are you going to tell him?

'You take your coffee black with three sugars, don't you?' she said the moment David had put down the phone. 'Personally I think it's a criminal waste of good coffee, but—'

'OK, talk, Rachel.'

'I thought that's what I was doing,' she said lightly, as she spooned some coffee into the cups and he crossed the room in two strides, his face angry.

'Will you stop being so damned brave, and noble, and *stupid*?'

'Stupid?' she repeated faintly. 'David—'

'Rachel, you are a lovely woman. A bright, clever, gifted woman, and when I think of what Greg's doing to you...' He cupped her face in his hands, forcing her to look up at him. 'Rachel, you have *got* to get yourself out of this situation. Oh, I know you're going to tell me you love him, and he loves you, but how can he love you if he's terrorising you, hurting you?'

There was anger in his voice and eyes, but his fingers were gentle, oh, so gentle, and a warm rush of heat flooded through her until she suddenly realised what he was saying.

'David, I'm not in love with Greg,' she protested. 'He's a horrible man.'

'He is?'

'He's a thief, and a bully—'

'OK, let's start this again,' he interrupted, his hands dropping to his sides, leaving her feeling oddly cold and bereft. 'If you hate him so much, why is he living with you, and why does he keep phoning you?'

'He doesn't live with me. He has a key to the house. Well, he did have one, but it doesn't work any more because I changed all the locks. Look, it's a long story,' she continued, seeing his confusion, 'and you don't have time to listen to it.'

'I'll make time.'

He would, too, judging by the look of grim determination on his face, and she gave in.

'When my aunt died I discovered she'd cut Greg out of her will, leaving her house and what little money she had to me, but what she didn't realise was that under Scots law she couldn't completely disinherit him. He was entitled to half her estate.'

'Why did she disinherit him?' he asked curiously, taking the cup of coffee she was holding out to him. 'Had they had a row or something?'

Rachel sighed. 'Greg started getting into trouble with the police when he was thirteen. Shoplifting, petty theft, that sort of thing. When he left school he moved on to bigger things, reselling stolen cars and housebreaking.'

'Didn't he ever get caught?'

'All the time. Greg's not what you'd call the brightest man in the world. He's a bully, and a thug, but not very bright. When he came out of prison three years ago, my aunt gave him an ultimatum. Either he changed his ways, or she didn't have a son any more.'

'I take it he didn't change his ways?'

She shook her head. 'When he found out about the will he was furious. I've given him all the money in his mother's bank account, and I'm trying to sell the house, but nobody wants it at the price he's asking. It's an old house, you see, and because Aunt Mary was always bailing Greg out of one mess after another, she never had any money left to treat the woodworm or the dry rot, or to replace the electrical wiring.'

'Have you told Greg this?'

'Until I'm blue in the face, but he thinks I'm deliberately

dragging my heels. He wants his money now, and he...'
She twisted the signet ring on her little finger. 'He has
very unpleasant ways of getting what he wants.'

His eyebrows snapped together. 'Maybe I should have
a little talk with your cousin Greg.'

'Over my dead body,' she said, considerably alarmed by
the steely glint that appeared in his blue eyes. 'The last
thing I want is you antagonising him.'

'I won't antagonise him, I'll simply sort him out.'

'Oh, no, you will not!' she spluttered. 'David, this is my
problem, not yours.'

'But he's harassing you.'

'And I'll deal with it,' she insisted. 'I don't need your
help.'

'I'm not saying you need it,' he retaliated. 'I'm saying
I want to do it. You're unhappy and frightened, and I can
help. I *want* to help.'

'*No*, David!'

'Dr Dunwoody, Mr Hart—the very people I'm looking
for,' Liz Baker declared, bouncing into the room with a
smile. Then she got a good look at both of them. 'Bad
time?'

'Not at all,' Rachel said with difficulty. 'What can we
do for you?'

'I was wondering if I could interest either of you in
some tickets for the July ball. It's a week on Saturday.'

'Dr Dunwoody doesn't go to dances,' David said, and
Liz glanced across at him, startled.

'But I thought you said—'

'She thinks they're really intended for the younger
members of staff.'

'I most certainly do not,' Rachel exclaimed, stung by
his implication that she was some sort of ancient crone
well past the age of dancing. 'And I'm perfectly capable
of speaking for myself, thank you very much.'

'It's going to be a terrific night out, Dr Dunwoody,' Liz
observed. 'Not only is it at the Grosvenor Hotel as usual,

but we've decided to make it a Famous People from History event.'

Rachel winced. It was bad enough that the Grosvenor Hotel always served the same finger buffet, and the music was always provided by the Blue Lagooners, but to spend an entire evening surrounded by people pretending to be Napoleon and Cleopatra? She'd rather have her legs waxed.

'I don't think a costume ball is quite Dr Dunwoody's thing,' David declared smoothly. 'In fact, I suspect she considers it rather silly.'

And since when had he decided she was some sort of staid, party-pooping killjoy? Rachel thought with a surge of anger. Well, she'd show him. Throwing him a look that spoke volumes, she reached for her handbag. 'How much are the tickets, Liz?'

'Forty pounds, Doctor, and it's really good value. There's just one thing I should perhaps mention—'

'Don't you have a consultation at half past three, Rachel?' David interrupted, and she swore as she caught sight of the time.

'Forty pounds, you said, Liz?' she confirmed, quickly pulling two £20 notes out of her purse, but when she'd given the sister the money and hurried out of the room, clutching her ticket, Liz turned to David with a troubled expression.

'You should have let me tell her about the draw.'

'She'll find out about it soon enough.'

'I suppose so, but… Look, do you think what you're doing is wise? I mean, you don't exactly seem to be Woody's flavour of the month at the moment.'

'I know what I'm doing, Liz.'

'I suppose you must,' the sister replied, 'but…' She shook her head ruefully. 'All I can say is I wouldn't want to be in your shoes when she discovers you're her date for the Famous People from History ball.'

CHAPTER FIVE

'I'M SORRY to drag you up here when you're just leaving for the day,' Annie said as Rachel hurried through the doors of Obs and Gynae. 'But Gideon's got his hands full with a pregnant RTA in A and E, Helen's in the middle of a breech, it's Tom's day off and—'

'It's no trouble,' Rachel insisted. 'David said if there were any problems in Obs and Gynae, I could come up and help. How far on is Mrs Dukakis?'

'Her waters broke in the ambulance, and her cervix is already fully dilated. It looks like it's going to be a fast birth but, given Mrs Dukakis's history and the fact she's gone into labour three weeks early…'

Rachel nodded. She'd heard all about Nana Dukakis. How the woman had come to Glasgow with her husband from a small village in Greece five months ago, and how neither of her two children had lived to see their second birthdays because they'd both been born with thalassaemia major, the inherited childhood anaemia.

'Have you notified the special care baby unit—told them the baby is going to need a complete blood transfusion when it's born?'

'They're on their way. In fact, I can't understand why they're not here already.'

A piercing yell broke the silence of the corridor, and the two women exchanged glances.

'Sounds like our mum-to-be is in good voice,' Rachel observed, and Annie grimaced.

'I'm afraid Mrs Dukakis's yells are the only thing you're going to be able to understand. She doesn't speak a word of English, as we discovered to our cost when she was brought into A and E as an emergency three months ago.'

'She was simply suffering from indigestion, wasn't she?' Rachel declared, and Annie nodded.

'Mark Lorimer—Tom's Australian friend who stood in for you while you were away—was a godsend. If he hadn't been able to speak Greek I don't know what we would have done.' Annie winced as yet another blood-curdling shriek split the air. 'I have to say I wish he was here now.'

So did Rachel after she'd spent just ten minutes in the delivery room.

'It's so frustrating,' she fumed. 'If I only knew the Greek words for "push" and "pant", it would help.'

'I think you're doing pretty well, considering,' Annie declared, seeing Rachel contort her face then mime a pushing motion.

'Pretty well's not good enough,' Rachel said as their patient bore down heavily, then let out an ear-splitting scream. 'Where's her husband—he speaks English, doesn't he?'

'The neighbours think he went out shopping, but— The baby's head's crowning, Rachel!'

'Where on earth is the SCBU team?' Rachel demanded, reaching out to support the baby's head. 'What are they coming by—banana boat?'

As though on cue, the door of the delivery room opened, and three heads appeared.

'Sorry for the delay, folks, but the lift's on the blink again, and we had to be rescued by Maintenance. How's our mum-to-be?'

'Almost a mum,' Rachel replied, turning the baby's head quickly. 'Terrific, Mrs Dukakis. You're doing wonderfully. Now, can you give me another big push?'

An unintelligible volley of Greek was her only reply, and Annie clasped hold of the woman's hand.

'Push, Mrs Dukakis. Push again, like this.' She screwed up her face as Rachel had done, and Mrs Dukakis pushed down again, and first one of the baby's shoulders emerged, then the other.

'Oh, wonderful, Mrs Dukakis,' Rachel exclaimed. 'Just one more—that's all it will need. You can do it,' she said as the woman shook her head. 'Honestly you can. Just give me one more really huge push.'

Mrs Dukakis took a deep breath, heaved with all her might and with a yell that matched its mother's the baby slid out into the world.

'It's a boy,' Annie said, tears shining in her eyes as Rachel clamped and cut the umbilical cord. 'Oh, Rachel, isn't he beautiful?'

Rachel had no time for anything but a brief glance. Mrs Dukakis was holding out her arms for her son, but the SCBU team was clearly already anxious to take the baby into their care.

'I know you want to hold him,' she said gently, seeing Mrs Dukakis's distress when her baby was placed in the medi-crib then whisked out of the delivery room. 'But he needs a blood transfusion, and you still have to deliver the placenta. I'm sorry. I wish I could explain it to you in your own language, but I can't,' she continued as tears welled in the woman's eyes. 'But your son is fine—he's fine.'

Or as fine as he could be with thalassaemia major, she thought when Mrs Dukakis slumped back down on the bed, tears trickling down her face.

'He looked so healthy,' Annie said when they were eventually able to leave Mrs Dukakis in Liz's capable hands. 'Healthy, and perfect, and *normal*.'

'I'm afraid all babies born with thalassaemia major do,' Rachel sighed. 'That's why so many of them die if their parents don't have access to modern medical facilities. Nobody realises they have an inherited disease, and their deaths are just put down to something else.'

'It must be awful,' Annie murmured. 'To carry a baby, feel it grow inside you, then give birth, only for the baby to die while it's just a toddler.'

'At least this baby has a chance,' Rachel declared. 'With monthly blood transfusions, and regular injections of Desferal to ensure its liver and kidneys aren't damaged, it should survive to adulthood.'

'I know, but…'

Her hand was resting protectively against her stomach, and Rachel reached out and hugged her. 'Hey, come on. Your baby is going to be fine.'

'I'm being stupid, aren't I?' Annie said with a wobbly smile. 'And the crazy thing is that when I first found out I was pregnant, all I could think was, Why now? Why do I have to be expecting a baby right now? Jamie's going to be starting school in August, and I'm finally going to be able to have some time to myself, and the thought of going back to nappies and bottles and sleepless nights…'

'I imagine quite a few second-time mums feel like that.' Rachel smiled, and Annie looked surprised.

'Do you think so?'

'Of course I do, and you being sick all the time can't have helped.'

'At least that's stopped now.'

She still didn't look any better, Rachel thought. She still looked pale, and tired, and at fourteen and a half weeks she should have begun to put on a little weight, but she hadn't.

'Annie—'

'I guess seeing Mrs Dukakis's baby, realising what its future is going to be, has put a lot of things into perspective for me. I'm so very lucky, aren't I?'

More than you know, Rachel thought wistfully as Annie hurried away in answer to Liz's beckoning wave. An awful lot more than you know.

'Well, hello, there, stranger. Are you working up here again, or just visiting?'

Rachel turned to see Helen smiling at her, and smiled back with an effort. 'Annie was a bit worried about Mrs Dukakis, so I came up to lend a hand. And before you ask, mum and her baby son are fine. I'm the one who's shattered.'

Helen laughed. 'I presume she still hasn't learned any more English?'

'Not a word. Have you ever tried miming "push" and "pant" to a woman in labour? By the time the baby was born I was wishing I was still on compassionate leave, and it was Mark Lorimer who was here instead of me.'

Helen's smile became oddly fixed. 'His linguistic skills certainly came in useful.'

'He seems to have been a big help all round,' Rachel commented. 'In fact, I've heard nothing but praise about him since I came back. Which is a bit lowering from my point of view,' she added with a chuckle, but Helen didn't laugh.

'You're every bit as talented as Mark Lorimer,' Helen said firmly.

'But not drop-dead gorgeous with black hair and green eyes,' Rachel said, her grey eyes twinkling. 'Half the nurses at the Belfield seem to have lost their hearts to him.'

'I wouldn't know.'

Rachel shot her a puzzled look. Normally, Helen was first with any interesting hospital gossip, but it was obvious she didn't want to talk about Mark Lorimer. Actually, now she came to think about it, Tom never wanted to talk about him either, which suggested something must have happened while she was away, but what?

'Helen—'

'I hear half the unmarried female staff want to tear your hair out because you've drawn David Hart as your partner for the ball tonight.'

Rachel wanted to say she'd happily swap partners with any of them but it would scarcely be tactful, so she said, 'I'm sure they'll have plenty of opportunities to dance with him.' In fact, she was prepared to bet money on it.

'Poor Liz is stuck with Sandy Fenton from Urology.'

'I hope she's bought a good pair of ear plugs,' Rachel

replied, momentarily distracted, but not for long. 'I just wish I hadn't bought a ticket, Helen. Dances aren't really my thing.'

'You'll love it,' the SHO insisted. 'Once you get there—get into the swing—I bet you'll have a terrific time.'

And pigs might fly, Rachel thought. She knew exactly what was going to happen tonight. David would escort her to the ball because he'd been unlucky enough to draw her ticket out of the hat, but that would be the last she'd see of him. Oh, he might stick with her for a couple of token dances and the finger buffet, but after that…wallflower time.

'Which historical person are you going as?' Helen continued as they came to a halt outside the door leading to the stairs.

'I've no idea. I haven't had a chance to visit the costume hire people yet.'

'You haven't had a chance…? Rachel, people have been hitting Kendra's in droves since they discovered it was to be a costume affair. The only matching costumes Tom and I could get were Anthony and Cleopatra, and we went to the shop five days ago.'

'I expect they'll have something left,' Rachel said dismissively, and Helen shook her head.

'Only the really boring ones like Florence Nightingale.'

As that was exactly what Rachel had planned on hiring, she changed the subject fast. 'You and Tom are going to the ball, then?'

'Wouldn't miss it for the world. I just hope the children don't play my mother up too much. John's at that age when he thinks he doesn't need a babysitter, and Emma…' The SHO shook her head. 'She's fed up being stuck in the house, bored with her physiotherapy exercises, and she wants Grandma to go home because she fusses too much.'

'Sounds like she's on the mend, then.' Rachel laughed, but she didn't feel much like laughing when she left Obs and Gynae and walked slowly down the stairs to the Mackenzie unit.

Everybody was excited about the ball. Pam and Annie had been talking about nothing else for days, giggling over the costumes they'd heard some of the staff had hired and longing for tonight. Only she seemed to be dreading it, wishing it was over.

Think yourself lucky, her mind pointed out. You could be in poor Liz Baker's shoes and landed with Sandy Fenton.

At least Sandy would stick with me for the evening, she thought gloomily as she pushed open the door of the unit. He might be the most boring man in the universe, but he would never escort her to a ball then leave her to prop up the wall while he danced the night away with a succession of nurses.

'Hey, cheer up. It might never happen,' David exclaimed as he came out of his consulting room.

It already has, she thought, but managed to smile. 'I'm just a little tired this afternoon, that's all,' she lied, and he grinned.

'Better get those energy levels up fast because I'm planning on us dancing the night away.'

Yeah, right. 'David, just because you drew my ticket doesn't mean either of us can't dance with other people,' she said, determined to appear magnanimous. 'In fact, I fully intend to.' Well, Gideon was bound to ask her for at least one dance. He was a gentleman as well as her boss, and Helen would probably lean on Tom to ask her as well.

'No way,' David said firmly. 'I've drawn you as my partner for the evening, and nobody's going to prise you from my side.'

He was kidding, wasn't he? 'David—'

'From the minute I pick you up this evening at a quarter to eight until the very last waltz, you're mine for the night.'

He meant it. Rachel could see from the glint in his eyes that he meant it, and she gulped. The ball was scheduled to last from eight o'clock in the evening until one in the morning. Five hours. Five hours of being whirled round the dance floor in his arms. Five hours of trying to make conversation with her head a mere six inches away from his.

Oh, cripes.

'I'm not much of a dancer,' she said desperately, and he smiled.

'No problem. I'll just hold onto you very tightly, and steer you in the right direction.'

He was going to hold onto her very tightly. As in holding her body close to his. As in moulding all his long, lean, muscular strength against her.

Oh, *cripes*.

'David—'

'Don't you want to know what my costume is?'

'Rasputin, the mad monk?' she suggested, and his lips quivered.

'Not even close. Dick Turpin, the highwayman.'

It sounded appropriate. Actually, it sounded very appropriate.

'What's your costume?' he asked.

Did any famous historical people wear bin liners? 'Wait and see,' she said.

'You *have* got one, haven't you?' he persisted. 'Because if you've left it to the last minute, Kendra's only going to be left with the really boring ones like—'

'Florence Nightingale,' Rachel finished for him dryly. 'Yes, I know.' She glanced down at her watch. It was a quarter to six. She had to get to Kendra's, and fast. 'Is it OK if I call it a day? I've one or two things to do before the ball tonight.'

He nodded, but as she began hurrying towards the staff-room to collect her coat, he called after her. 'Can't wait to see what you're wearing tonight.'

You and me both, she thought grimly. You and me both.

*   *   *

'But you *must* have something left,' Rachel said desperately as the assistant in Kendra's shook her head. 'I'll take anything. Boadicea, King Kong, anything.'

The girl began to shake her head again, then stopped. 'Actually, we *do* have two costumes left. The ladies who looked at them this morning weren't sure if they were suitable and said they were going to try the costume-hire shop in Sauchiehall Street. They told me that if they weren't back by five o'clock I was to hire them out, and it's well past five now.' She gazed at Rachel appraisingly. 'You're a size twelve, aren't you?'

On a good day, Rachel thought, but she was going to squeeze into one of these costumes if it killed her. No way was she going to have David think she'd chickened out, deliberately waited until the last possible minute so all the costumes had been hired and she couldn't go.

'This is all we have left, Doctor,' the assistant declared as she re-emerged from the back shop. 'The Florence Nightingale...'

Which looked exactly as Rachel had pictured it. Long, grey, high-necked, and... Boring. There was even a cap and a tiny pretend lamp to go with it so if the dress didn't cool any man's ardour, those two accessories most certainly would.

'What's the other costume?' she asked.

'The Nell Gwynn. She was one of Charles the Second's many mistresses. Apparently he caught sight of her selling oranges outside Covent Garden theatre in London and, bingo, he was hooked.'

If Nell had been wearing a dress like the one the assistant was holding up for her, Rachel wasn't surprised. It was stunning. Made of copper taffeta with a wide, floorlength, sweeping skirt and a neckline embroidered with tiny blue rosettes, she couldn't for the life of her understand why anybody would have had second thoughts about hiring it.

'Wait until you try it on.' The girl chuckled when

Rachel voiced her surprise. 'It's the neckline, you see. It's a bit…well, it's a bit revealing.'

Revealing wasn't the word, Rachel thought with dismay when the assistant had helped her into the costume. It was practically indecent.

'I don't suppose it comes with a lace collar or something?' she said, gazing at her reflection, appalled.

'I'm afraid not. There's a fan…'

Which was nowhere near big enough, Rachel decided, not when the costume's built-in corset had hitched her breasts up so high they looked in danger of spilling out.

She couldn't wear this. Not in public. And certainly not to a ball with David Hart. The shop in Sauchiehall Street would be closed by now so it would have to be the Florence Nightingale. All right, people might snigger at her for choosing something so safe and boring, but better them sniggering than for her to have to pop their eyeballs back in all night.

'Would you like to try on the Florence Nightingale?' the girl said, clearly reading her mind, and Rachel glanced over her shoulder at the dress.

Lord, but it looked so drab and boring. Like my own life, she realised, and suddenly she felt belligerent.

Why should she go dressed to the ball as a buttoned-up Victorian lady, when what she really wanted to wear was the dress of a seventeenth-century courtesan? Nobody would be surprised if she came as Florence Nightingale. They'd just think, Typical Woody. Stiff and starchy, the very epitome of Victorian womanhood—but if she came as Nell Gwynn…

'I don't want to hurry you, Doctor,' the assistant continued, 'but I'm supposed to shut the shop at six, and it's already a quarter past.'

OK, so the neckline was a little low—a *little*? But the dress was so very beautiful. And she looked like a stranger in it. A stunning, sexy, voluptuous stranger.

'Doctor…?'

David hadn't been sorry when she'd left him all those years ago. He'd been irritated, and annoyed, and piqued, so why shouldn't she let him see what he'd lost when she'd walked away? He'd done nothing but try to flirt with her ever since he'd come back into her life, so why couldn't she flirt with him and tease *him* all night? She would be safe in the knowledge that they were surrounded by three hundred people and, though he might look, he couldn't touch.

'Doctor…'

'I'll take it,' she said quickly, and the girl smiled.

'A very wise decision if I may say so. Believe me, that dress is going to knock his socks off.'

It had better, Rachel thought as the girl wrapped up the dress, because if David took one look at her and laughed he'd be a dead duck.

David didn't sound to be in a laughing mood when he rang her doorbell at exactly a quarter to eight that evening. In fact, from the sustained pressure he was exerting on her unfortunate doorbell, he sounded edgy and impatient.

Keep him waiting, she told herself, pinning the last of the ringlets she'd curled her hair up into against the side of her head. If you want to show him what he's been missing for the last six years, keep him waiting.

The doorbell rang again, even more stridently, and she took a last look at her reflection and smiled. She looked good. Well, maybe good was the wrong word, she thought with a chuckle. Wanton. Wanton, and sexy, and now was the time to find out if David agreed with her.

'What took you so long?' he protested as she opened her front door. 'I thought…'

'You thought what?' she asked as he came to a sudden halt.

For a second he said nothing. For an even longer second he simply stared at her, then he swallowed convulsively. 'Rachel, you look…'

'Sensational, incredible, dynamite?' she suggested.

'All three, and then some.' He nodded. 'But you're not— You can't seriously be meaning to go to the ball in that.'

'What's wrong with it?' she asked, gazing down at herself, then up at him innocently.

'Rachel, your breasts—that dress— Hell's bells, I can practically see all the way down to your navel!'

'I know it's a little low-cut…'

'*A little!*'

'But it's a party, and I don't think there's any harm in showing a bit of flesh at a party, do you?' she said blithely, and thought he was going to explode.

'Rachel—'

'You look very nice,' she said. Actually, he looked devastatingly handsome in his ruffled white shirt, green velvet knee breeches and matching green velvet tail coat. Like one of the characters in the Regency romances she so enjoyed reading. The ones that made her toes curl and her body feel hot inside. Rather like the way she was feeling right now, she realised. 'If the ball starts at eight, shouldn't we be going?' she said quickly.

'Going?' he repeated. 'You mean you're actually going out in public like that?'

'Of course I am.'

'But, Rachel, you can't,' he gasped, his colour high. 'My lord, do you have any idea of how you look?'

'That good, eh?'

'Rachel, every man at the ball is going to be crawling all over you.'

'In that case, what are we waiting for?' she said, sweeping past him and down to his car.

'But, Rachel—'

'Look, are you coming or not?' she demanded, glancing back at him over her shoulder.

And though he muttered something which sounded suspiciously like, 'God in heaven,' he followed her.

So did half the unmarried men who worked at the Belfield when she arrived at the Grosvenor Hotel. In fact, from the minute she walked in, she was surrounded. Men who had passed her in the hospital corridors since she'd joined the staff two years ago without even so much as a good morning now clamoured for a dance, and to David's clear fury she accepted every invitation with alacrity.

'Don't you think the poor bloke's suffered enough?' Gideon asked halfway through the evening as he whirled her round the room in a fast foxtrot.

'Suffered?' she repeated, staring up at him in wide-eyed innocence, and he laughed.

'Woody, whatever he's done, I think you've paid him back in triplicate, don't you?'

Not yet, she thought. Not by a long shot. OK, so maybe the evening hadn't turned out quite as she'd planned, and instead of flirting with David she'd ended up flirting with everybody else, including Mr Aren't-I-Wonderful himself, Lawrence Summers, the consultant in charge of Men's Surgical, but knowing David had been watching her while she did it was just as satisfying.

But there was clearly a limit to his forbearance, and when the master of ceremonies announced the final dance of the evening, David strode up to her, his face determined.

'OK, you've danced with every damn member of staff, including the hospital janitor, and this one's mine.'

'Why, of course.' She beamed. 'You only needed to ask.'

He gave her a long hard look, then the corners of his mouth quirked. 'You've done this on purpose, haven't you? Deliberately set out to make yourself look as sexy as possible.'

'Did I succeed?' she couldn't resist saying, and he drew her into his arms as the Blue Lagooners began to play the last waltz.

'Of course you did,' he growled. 'But now it's my turn. When I take you home after this dance, it's my turn.'

Did he mean what she thought he meant? She shivered slightly but in truth she didn't care any more. Maybe it was the night, or the Nell Gwynn costume, or the way David had been scowling at her all evening, but she felt reckless, and exciting, and different. Tomorrow she would go back to being her old dull, boring self again, but to-night...

Her light-headedness lasted all the way home in the car. It was still there when he followed her into her house, and it was only when he took her in his arms and kissed her that she felt the first vague stirrings of doubt.

'David, I think perhaps this might be a mistake,' she gasped, half-heartedly trying to extricate herself from his arms.

'Now she tells me,' he murmured, kissing the palm of her hand, sending a rush of heat fluttering through her stomach.

'No, I mean it,' she insisted. 'I really don't think—'

'I don't think you should either,' he said huskily. 'To-night's not a night for thinking.'

He was right, she thought as he drew her back into his arms and kissed her again, this time taking her breath away so completely that all she could do was enjoy the heat and shudder that raced through her. It was a night for making love. A night to be taken, and enjoyed, and she wanted it, wanted all of it.

Oh, do that again, she thought dizzily when his lips left hers and planted a searing row of kisses along the neckline of her gown. Touch me there again, she thought when his tongue curled enticingly between the crease in her breasts, and she heard him chuckle and duly oblige though she hadn't said a word.

How did he know just where to touch, where to kiss her? she wondered as he threaded his fingers through her hair, locking her lips to his. How did he know just what to do to send the blood rushing to her head and her body flooding with need?

Practice, her mind whispered. All he's doing is putting his skills into practice. It doesn't have to be you. It could be any woman in his arms, and the thought had her surfacing breathlessly.

'David, this…this really is a very bad idea.'

'On the contrary, I think it's an excellent idea,' he replied, easing down her bodice so her breasts spilled out into his hands, his eyes dark, liquid, needy.

She did, too, when he bent his head to take one of her nipples into his mouth and her stomach jolted in response, but she shouldn't—she knew that she shouldn't.

'David, we're not…' Oh, lord, *yes*, she thought as he began suckling her, biting gently down on the nipple, then licking it with his tongue. 'We're not the same people we were before.'

'Even better,' he said, turning his attention to her other breast, making her squirm and arch, so she could feel him pulsing against her. 'We can compare the differences and the similarities. You can show me the birthmark on your tummy, and I'll show you—'

'But we mustn't,' she said faintly. 'I mustn't…'

'Oh, come on, Rachel, we're good together,' he whispered into her neck, his voice deep, and dark, and sensual. 'You must remember how good we are together.'

She did. Only he had ever been able to make her feel this way. Only he had ever been able to turn her bones to jelly and her blood into molten fire, surging and throbbing with life, and she was falling, falling into him. Feeling his heat, his desire, feeling the same way herself. Lord, but she wanted him. Oh, yes—*yes*, she thought as his hand slid up under her dress, caressing her inner thigh, the curve of her bottom, before he slipped his fingers inside her panties and began stroking her.

'You always did like that, didn't you?' He laughed as she convulsed against him when he eased his fingers deep inside her, and an icy chill ran down her spine.

He was right, and that was why this was so wrong. She

was reliving the past. He hadn't changed. He was still the same man he'd been six years ago, and just as he hadn't been willing to give her what she'd wanted then, he wouldn't be able to give it to her now.

'David…' With a supreme effort of will she pulled herself out of his arms. 'I don't want to make love with you.'

He stared at her in confusion for a second, looking as dazed as she felt, then grinned. 'Your ears are burning again.'

They weren't the only part. All of her was burning, melting, wanting to open herself to him, wanting the kind of love-making only he could give, except that it wouldn't be making love for him. It never had been.

'All you want is sex,' she said bleakly.

'And you don't?' He stared down at her erect, throbbing nipples, the colour that was suffusing her cheeks, and shook his head. 'Whopper, Rachel.'

'OK, so maybe I do want you,' she faltered, pulling the bodice of her dress back up over her breasts, 'but people don't always act on what they want, and I'm not going to.'

'Why on earth not?' he protested.

'Because I don't want—or need—any complications in my life, and that's what you'd be. So, attractive though you are, I think I'll pass.'

'You make me sound like something on offer on a sweet counter,' he said indignantly. 'I'm talking—'

'A two- or three-month fling if I'm lucky, and then off you go?' She shook her head. 'Sorry, not interested.'

'Rachel—'

'Good sex isn't enough any more, David.'

'What more can there be?' he exclaimed. 'Good sex is fun, and we always had fun together.'

They had, but making love, enjoying one another's bodies, had always been just fun to him. All those stolen afternoons in her little flat, the long drives out to the country where they'd made love under the stars, they'd all been nothing but fun to him.

Actually, the way her body was reacting, it sounded pretty much like fun to do it again, too, but... Her mind sheared off fast. Don't go that way. Not again.

'I happen to think there ought to be more to a relationship than just fun,' she said, and he gazed at her blankly. He didn't understand. She doubted if he ever would, and she said the words she knew would have him leaving before she'd even finished. 'I want commitment, David.'

His eyes slid away from hers. 'I don't do commitment, you know that.'

'Which is why we stop this right now,' she said. 'David, I'll be thirty next month, and I want stability in my life. I want a partner and a baby, and that's not you, is it?'

For a second he said nothing, then his lips creased into one of his megawatt smiles. 'I don't suppose there's any chance we could discuss this after we'd made love?'

She closed her eyes, shutting him out. 'David, go away.'

'Go?' he echoed. 'But I thought—'

'I know what you thought, and it isn't going to happen.'

'But—'

'David, just *go*.'

He did. She heard the sound of his feet echoing down the hall, then the front door opening, and when it closed she walked slowly over to the sofa and sat down.

She'd done the right thing. Showing David the door had been the right thing to do. It proved she was nobody's fool any more, that she'd matured.

Making love with him would have been even better, her body telegraphed, and she shook her head. No, it wouldn't. OK, so her body was still aching for him, but her heart, her mind...

'Been there, done that,' she told the empty room. 'And where did it get me?'

Nowhere alley, that's where. David was always going

to walk away from commitment, and she hadn't wanted that six years ago, and she didn't want it now. She wanted…

I want him to love me, she realised with a sudden depressing flash of insight. Fool that I am, I gave him my heart six years ago, and I still want him to fall in love with me, and it isn't going to happen.

So I was right to tell him to go, she told herself as she curled up on the sofa and hugged a cushion to her chest. I was right to tell him to leave.

But it would still have been good to have him back again, her body sighed. To have him fill me, and satisfy me as he did so often in the past.

It would still have been good.

GET FREE BOOKS and a FREE MYSTERY GIFT WHEN YOU PLAY THE...

Just scratch off the silver box with a coin. Then check below to see the gifts you get!

SLOT MACHINE GAME!

YES! I have scratched off the silver box. Please send me the four FREE books and mystery gift for which I qualify. I understand I am under no obligation to purchase any books, as explained on the back of this card. I am over 18 years of age.

M3KI

Mrs/Miss/Ms/Mr   Initials

BLOCK CAPITALS PLEASE

Surname

Address

Postcode

Worth **FOUR FREE BOOKS** plus a **BONUS** Mystery Gift!

Worth **FOUR FREE BOOKS!**

Worth **ONE FREE BOOK!**

TRY AGAIN!

Visit us online at www.millsandboon.co.uk

The Reader Service™ — Here's how it works:

Accepting the free books places you under no obligation to buy anything. You may keep the books and gift and return the despatch note marked 'cancel'. If we do not hear from you, about a month later we'll send you 6 brand new books and invoice you just £2.60* each. That's the complete price - there is no extra charge for postage and packing. You may cancel at any time, otherwise every month we'll send you 6 more books, which you may either purchase or return to us - the choice is yours.

*Terms and prices subject to change without notice.

NO STAMP NEEDED!

THE READER SERVICE™
FREE BOOK OFFER
FREEPOST CN81
CROYDON
CR9 3WZ

NO STAMP
NECESSARY
IF POSTED IN
THE U.K. OR N.I.

CHAPTER SIX

RACHEL put her head down on her desk and groaned as the consultant from Men's Surgical swept out of her consulting room, slamming the door shut behind him. Well, that was yet another member of staff who would be cutting her dead from now on. Not that Lawrence Summers had ever deigned to talk to her before, but he most definitely wouldn't be stopping by for a chat in the future.

'Mr Summers didn't look a happy camper.' Annie grinned as she stuck her head round the door.

'Lawrence Summers can go strangle himself with his own ego,' Rachel exclaimed. 'Him and all the other jerks who've swanned in here this morning. Just who the hell do they think they are, Annie? Not one of them has exchanged more than two words with me since I came to the Belfield, and now just because they discovered on Saturday that I've got breasts—'

'And in a big way.'

'They turn up here on Monday morning, expecting me to say, yes, sir, thank you kindly, sir, I'd love to go out with you, sir. The creeps.'

Annie laughed as she shut the door. 'But surely you must have realised when you wore that dress on Saturday that you'd have every wolf in the hospital beating a path to your door?'

'I didn't—honestly I didn't,' Rachel protested. 'I only wore it because it was either that or the Florence Nightingale, and David said the Florence Nightingale was boring.'

'I see.'

'Helen said it was boring, too,' Rachel hurried on, as

97

she watched the laughter fade from the junior doctor's face, 'and it was boring, and drab, and… Oh, dammit, Annie, I know the Nell Gwynn was far too revealing, but it was so pretty, and I wanted…I wanted to make an impact.'

'You certainly did that.'

'I just didn't realise it was going to make such an impact on so many men,' Rachel said unhappily. 'I only wanted… I just hoped—'

'It would make an impact on David,' Annie finished for her with a sigh. 'Oh, Rachel…'

'I know—I know. It was stupid—childish. And it's not as though I want to get involved with him again, because I don't, but—'

'You just wanted to show him what he'd lost,' Annie nodded. 'I understand.'

Rachel fiddled with the paperweight on her desk, then forced herself to meet Annie's gaze. 'Dumb, wasn't I?'

'Human, I'd say.'

'No, dumb. Just plain dumb.'

'Did…?' Annie paused, and it was her turn to fiddle with the paperweight. 'Did it work?'

'Rather too well, actually,' Rachel said ruefully, and Annie looked even more troubled.

'Rachel, I love my brother dearly, but he's not—'

'Reliable, or faithful, or into permanent relationships. I *know*, Annie. Which is why Saturday was such a big mistake.'

And it had been. Lord, she was still squirming at the thought of how she'd behaved after David had taken her home, and worst of all was the knowledge that she'd have to face him again.

What could she say to him—what would he say to her? Luckily he'd gone straight to the operating theatre when he'd arrived this morning, but she couldn't avoid him for ever. At some point they would meet, and then what?

Her aunt would have said that any woman who behaved

as she had on Saturday night—deliberately setting out to tantalise and flirt with a man and then showing him the door—was no better than a tease. David would undoubtedly have come up with a much harsher label by now, and he would be right.

'Rachel…' Annie gazed at her uncertainly for a second, then clearly made up her mind. 'Look, I don't normally interfere in my brother's private life, but would you like me to speak to him?'

'And say what?' Rachel demanded. 'That Rachel Dunwoody got herself in way over her head on Saturday and she's sorry? I don't think that would help, Annie.'

'Perhaps not, but—'

Rachel's intercom crackled into life, and she reached to answer it.

'Sorry about this, Rachel,' Pam announced, 'but Theatre's phoned to say Mr Hart's going to be another half-hour with his op, so can you take his half-past twelve appointment with Rhona Scott?'

'Oh, brilliant,' Rachel groaned when the intercom went dead. 'If there's one person I'd rather not see this morning, it's Rhona.'

'You're going to be giving her bad news?' Annie said, and Rachel shook her head.

'It isn't what you or I might consider bad news, but somehow I don't think Rhona will agree.'

'Tom performed a cornual anastomosis on her back in April, didn't he?' Annie observed. 'To unblock one of her Fallopian tubes?'

Rachel nodded. 'Tom's quietly confident she'll conceive without our help, but I'm afraid Rhona's not what you'd call a patient woman, and I think she's going to demand *in vitro* fertilisation treatment.'

Rhona did.

'Look, Rhona, it's not a question of what *you* want,' Rachel said gently when the woman declared that three months was long enough to wait to see if her operation had been a success, and as it plainly hadn't she wanted to try IVF. 'It can take a year for your body to adjust after such major surgery—'

'If it's a question of money, I can pay for the treatment,' Rhona insisted. 'My husband and I could take out a second mortgage on our house. I'm sure the lenders would agree, and—'

'Rhona, you're not listening to me,' Rachel interrupted. 'The operation you've had has a fifty per cent chance of success. That means you have a one in two chance of conceiving normally. IVF, on the other hand, is not only one of the most demanding and emotionally fraught treatments you can undergo, but it also comes with only a one in eight chance of you giving birth to a baby at the end of it.'

'But the newspapers say—'

'The newspapers want to sell papers, Rhona. They know there's a lot of unhappy women out there who'll buy anything with the headline IVF, THE MIRACLE TREATMENT, but believe me, it's the last resort for infertile couples, and something you should undertake only after a great deal of thought.'

Rhona gazed at her uncertainly for a moment, then shook her head. 'I want to see the new man—Mr Hart. I was supposed to see him today anyway, not you. He's the infertility expert, so I want to see him.'

'Mr Hart's been delayed in the operating theatre—'

'Then I want to make another appointment—one when I *will* see him.'

Rhona's face was pale but determined, and Rachel sighed. 'If that's what you want, I can arrange it, but I have to say Mr Hart is only going to repeat what I've already told you. That you haven't waited long enough to see if your operation was a success. All we're asking is for you to wait a year—'

'How old are you, Doctor?'

'I'll be thirty next month. And before you ask, no, I

don't have any children,' Rachel continued quickly, guessing what was coming next, 'but I do know how you're feeling—'

'No, you don't. You might think you do,' Rhona said as Rachel tried to interrupt, 'but you don't. I was a careerwoman, like you—a real high-flier, travelling the world, dealing in high finance—until I met my husband. Do you believe in love at first sight, Doctor?'

'I…well…' Of course she did. The very first time she'd seen David walking down the corridor at the Hebden she'd fallen for him, hook, line and sinker. 'Yes—yes, I do.'

'That's how it was for Simon and me,' Rhona said, tears welling in her eyes. 'When we got married I thought I had it all. A husband who loved me, a good job, a nice home. I only wanted one more thing to make our lives complete.'

'Rhona—'

'I'm thirty-six, doctor, and my husband and I have been trying for a baby for six years. Six years of waiting, and hoping, and then crying every time my period starts because another month has gone by and I'm still not pregnant, only another month older. Six years of trying not to show the envy and the hatred—yes, the *hatred*—I feel when my friends tell me they're pregnant for the second or third time. There's no way you can understand that, Doctor. Only somebody in my situation could.'

Rachel reached for Rhona's hands and clasped them tightly in hers. 'You're right. I don't understand—and it was very wrong of me to say that I did, but, Rhona, I truly—*truly*—believe that your best chance of conceiving is to wait.'

The woman stared at her blindly, and for a second Rachel thought she was going to agree, then she shook her head. 'I want to make an appointment to see Mr Hart.'

There was no point in arguing. Rhona had clearly decided that if she saw David he would start her on IVF, and then all her troubles would be over.

If only it was that easy, Rachel thought with a deep sigh

after Rhona had gone, but it wasn't. She'd worked in Obs and Gynae long enough to know nothing was ever simple. All she could do was tell Pam to make Rhona another appointment, and then keep a careful check on her to make sure she didn't slip into depression.

Except that she wouldn't be able to keep a check on her for very long, because in less than two months she'd be back working in Obs and Gynae.

You can always come up to the unit occasionally, she told herself. Ask how Rhona's doing. And Sable Mitchell, and all the other women you've seen in the past month. But it wouldn't be the same, she realised as she put Rhona's file into her out-tray. Not the same as actually seeing them, working through their treatments with them, rejoicing with them if they became pregnant.

Oh, lord, now she was getting depressed, she thought ruefully, and it was silly. Infertility treatment might be interesting, and challenging, but she was an obs and gynae specialist registrar. It was what she was trained for, and to change specialities now...

Lunch, she told herself firmly. What she needed was lunch. Everything always looked brighter after a meal, even if the meal was just the two cheese and salad sandwiches she'd picked up from the canteen. Quickly she walked out into the corridor, only to come to a very fast halt.

David was standing outside his consulting room, and if she didn't duck back into her own room quickly he'd see her. Wimp, her heart mocked. Better a wimp than a very unpleasant scene, she decided, but she was too late. He'd already turned and seen her.

'Hi, sexy.'

Hi, *sexy*? Was he being sarcastic? He certainly didn't look as though he was intending to be, but...

'I don't think that's very funny,' she said, and it was his turn to look bewildered.

'Funny? I wasn't trying to be funny.'

'Then, what's with the "Hi, sexy"?' she demanded.

'Well, "hi" is a shortened Americanism for hello, and "sexy"—'

'I know what the words mean,' she exclaimed. 'What I want to know is why you're saying them to me.'

'Well, "hi" because it's the first time I've seen you this morning, and "sexy"…' A smile crept into his deep blue eyes. 'Judging by the number of male members of staff who seem to have been falling over themselves to visit the Mackenzie unit today, I'd say it was pretty appropriate, wouldn't you?'

So word about the wolves at her door had travelled all the way down to the operating theatre, had it? Stupid observation. Of course it had. You couldn't change your underwear at the Belfield without everybody knowing.

'David—'

'Though I have to say,' he continued, 'I still think your hair is much prettier loose than up in that awful bun.'

'It's a French pleat, and I wear my hair like this so it doesn't get in the way when I'm working, and…' And what the hell was she doing, discussing French pleats? Take the bull by the horns, Rachel. Apologise for what happened on Saturday night after the ball, and hope to heaven he can forgive you. 'David, about what happened on Saturday—'

'You said you weren't much of a dancer,' he protested. 'Talk about hiding your light under a bushel.'

'I'm not talking about the dance,' she interrupted. 'I'm talking about what happened afterwards, when you took me home and…' Lord, but this was mortifying, but it had to be said. 'It was my fault. What happened was my fault. I was wrong to lead you on—'

'Forget it.'

Forget it?

He was still smiling at her. In fact, if anything his smile had widened. Surely he couldn't still be trying to flirt with her? Not after what she'd said to him at the weekend?

Rachel squared her shoulders and looked him straight in the eye, determined there would be no misunderstanding. 'David, what I said to you on Saturday about not wanting any more flings, but wanting a partner and a baby and commitment…I meant it.'

'I know.'

'So there's no point in you trying to flirt with me any more. I can't—and I won't—get involved with you again. Do…do you understand?' she continued uncertainly as he kept on smiling. One of his big, open, got-to-love-me smiles.

'Of course I do. Just as I also know it's up to me to make you change your mind.'

To make her change her mind? She gazed at him in disbelief. Hadn't he heard anything she'd said? 'David, listen to me—'

'You'll be pleased to know Jennifer Norton's blood pressure is much better this morning. It's nowhere near normal yet, but the magnesium sulphate seems to be helping. She'll be out in a minute if you want to talk to her,' he continued, gesturing towards his consulting room. 'I'm just giving her a little privacy while she gets dressed.'

He was deliberately changing the subject. Probably regrouping his forces while he tried to figure out some other strategy to get her into his bed, she thought angrily. Well, he could regroup all he liked, it wasn't going to get him anywhere..

'David—'

'Have you heard the good news, Dr Dunwoody?' Jennifer declared as she emerged from David's consulting room, all smiles. 'My scan's perfect, and my blood pressure's actually gone down a little bit.'

'I'm very pleased to hear it,' Rachel replied with difficulty, and Jennifer beamed up at David.

'And it's all down to Mr Hart. He's wonderful, isn't he, Dr Dunwoody?'

'Terrific,' Rachel said grimly, and saw a disconcerting gleam of amusement appear on David's face.

'Don't forget to make another appointment with our receptionist before you leave,' he said as Jennifer hitched her shoulder-bag across her shoulder. 'I want to see you in a month's time for your next injection, and—'

'If I notice the swelling in my ankles and thighs getting worse, I'm to come back right away.' Jennifer nodded. 'I won't forget, Mr Hart.'

'See that you don't,' he said. 'We want you in tip-top shape before you have your babies.'

'Like Dr Dunwoody,' Jennifer observed. 'Oh, I don't mean you're pregnant, Doctor,' she continued hurriedly when Rachel looked puzzled, 'just that I've noticed you've been looking really good recently. Working in infertility must suit you.'

'It's not the work, Jennifer.' David winked. 'It's me. My charm, my wit and incredible modesty.'

Jennifer shook her head and laughed. 'How on earth do you put up with this man, Dr Dunwoody? He's the most terrible flirt.'

'Oh, I just take him round the back of the hospital occasionally and hose him down with cold water,' Rachel replied, and Jennifer laughed again.

'You know, I think you might have met your match, Mr Hart,' she said, and David glanced across at Rachel, a faint smile in his gaze.

'You could be right.'

He was doing it again, Rachel thought with irritation, all too aware that her cheeks were reddening, and even more annoyingly aware that Jennifer was glancing from her to David with keen interest. What did she have to do to get him to believe her? Write 'I'm not interested in you' on a placard and carry it around with her wherever she went?

'I'm afraid you'll have to excuse me,' she said swiftly. 'It's after one o'clock—'

'Is it?' Jennifer gasped. 'Cripes, I must be making tracks, too. My husband always thinks there's something wrong with the babies if I'm late back from the hospital.'

'Don't forget to make your next appointment,' David called after her as she began hurrying away. 'Same time, same place, four weeks from today.'

'I'll remember,' Jennifer replied.

When she'd disappeared through the swing doors at the end of the corridor, he said, 'Nice woman.'

'Most people are,' Rachel observed.

'Me included?'

His eyes were fixed on her, quizzical, teasing, and her heart sank. Why had she ever worn that damned dress? If only she hadn't worn that dress she could have dismissed what he was doing as flirting, but it wasn't flirting any more, not after Saturday. Not after she'd let him touch her where he shouldn't have touched, kissed him back with a fervour to match his own. She was the one who'd given him the green light, and now she was having to pay for it.

'Lunch,' she said with difficulty. 'There's not much of our lunch-hour left so I think we should grab our sandwiches while we can.'

'Sounds good to me,' he replied, falling into step beside her as she headed for the staffroom. 'Any problems this morning?'

Only one if she didn't count his unsettling presence and the way she'd been besieged by every sleaze-ball in the Belfield since she'd come on duty. 'Rhona Scott would like an appointment to see you as soon as possible.'

'What on earth for?' he demanded, and when she explained, he shook his head. 'Tell Pam to make her another appointment—for next week if it's possible so we can sort this out once and for all—but Rhona's going to be one very unhappy lady when she sees me. Three months is nowhere near long enough for us to know whether her operation was successful or not, and as for wanting to try IVF...'

'That's what I told her,' Rachel said as they walked into the staffroom and David switched on the kettle, 'but I have to admit I feel a certain sympathy for her. She knows I'm not an infertility specialist, so she's bound to wonder if I might be wrong.'

'You're not.'

'I know, but…' She shuddered as he took a bite out of one of his salami and pickle and mayonnaise rolls. 'How *can* you eat that stuff?'

He smiled. 'It's lovely. Want to try?'

She grimaced. 'I'll stick with my cheese and salad sandwiches.'

'You don't eat enough.'

'David.'

'OK, OK. None of my business. What you told Rhona about IVF and her tubal surgery was absolutely spot on, so stop underestimating your medical ability. I've told you before that you'd make an excellent infertility specialist registrar.'

'"Would make"—as in the future, if I changed specialities,' she argued back, 'but right now I'm winging it. I know it, even if you don't, and this unit needs—deserves—somebody considerably more experienced than me.'

'We're managing.'

'Managing isn't good enough,' she insisted. 'For a brand-new unit like this you need fully qualified staff. The patients deserve it, and so do you, and I, for one, will be a whole lot happier when you've interviewed and appointed your permanent staff.'

'Do you want tea or coffee?'

'Coffee, please.' He took two cups out of the cupboard, and as she watched him she noticed a distinctly suspicious wash of colour creeping up the back of his neck. 'You *have* set up the interviews, haven't you, David?'

'Not exactly…'

'But you promised you'd do them two weeks ago,' she

protested. 'You said you were on the case, that everything was in hand, and now you're telling me you haven't done anything?'

'There's plenty of time,' he said, spooning some coffee into the two cups, and she shook her head at him with exasperation.

'David, this unit needs two specialist registrars and an SHO, minimum. What if the first batch of candidates you interview turn out to be hopeless, and you have to advertise again? I'm supposed to be going back to Obs and Gynae at the beginning of September—that's less than two months away.'

'You could change your mind.'

She drew herself up to her full five feet six. 'David, read my lips. I am not—repeat, *not*—going to change my mind.'

'You might.'

'David—'

'Oh, good, Rachel.' Pam smiled as she came into the staffroom. 'I've been looking for you.'

'If it's about my time sheet,' Rachel began uncomfortably, 'I'll do it today.'

'It's nothing to do with your time sheet,' the receptionist said, 'though if you could get it done some time today Admin would really appreciate it. It's the embargo on telephone calls from your cousin.'

'Embargo?' Rachel repeated blankly. 'What embargo?'

'The one Mr Hart issued a fortnight ago when he said I wasn't to put any calls from your cousin through to you.'

Rachel's eyes shot across to David who suddenly seemed to be finding the contents of the coffee-cups inordinately fascinating. 'How many of these telephone calls have there been?'

'Twelve, thirteen—something like that,' Pam said. 'I'm afraid I can't remember exactly because I've been putting the phone down on him. He's such a very unpleasant person. So, do you want me to keep the embargo in place, or…?'

Part of her longed to tell the receptionist to remove the embargo immediately, but the other part—the wimpy part…

'Keep it in place,' she muttered, and because it wasn't the receptionist's fault she added quickly, 'Thanks, Pam.'

'No trouble, Doctor.'

Not yet there isn't, Rachel thought as the woman left, but there was going to be. There was most definitely going to be, she decided as she watched David carry the two cups of coffee over to the coffee-table and sit down.

'Now, before you start,' he said, glancing up at her, 'I was only—'

'Interfering in my private life,' she said, keeping her temper with difficulty. 'I *told* you I didn't need your help. I *told* you I'd deal with it myself.'

'But you weren't dealing with it, were you?' he said in such a reasonable tone that she longed to kick his shins. 'All you were doing was refusing to take his calls, so I've simply saved you the trouble.'

'That is not the point,' she said through clenched teeth. 'The point is, it was *my* problem. Mine to sort out and deal with, not yours. All you've done with your high-handed interference is antagonise him, and now he's going to start phoning me at home again. In fact, I'm amazed he hasn't started already.'

'He can't. I phoned the telephone operator and asked them to put a call divert on your home phone so every time he rings they intercept the call.'

Her mouth opened and closed soundlessly for a second, then she exploded. 'You did *what*?'

'There's no need to thank me,' he said airily. 'It was my pleasure.'

She gritted her teeth until they hurt. 'Now, listen here, David, and listen good. My private life is my own. If I have a problem *I* deal with it, and I do not need—or want—you interfering in things that don't concern you.'

'But this does concern me,' he protested. 'You were being harassed, you were unhappy—'

'What do I have to do to get you to listen to me?' she said with frustration. 'Which part of the words "Keep out of my private life" don't you understand?'

'Rachel—'

'I do not *want* your help. I do not *need* your help—'

'Boy, but I could really murder a cup of coffee,' Annie said as she came into the staffroom. She glanced from Rachel to David, said, 'And then again perhaps not,' and backed out the door fast.

'Rachel, all I've done is stop Greg harassing you,' David declared. 'It's what you wanted, wasn't it?'

It was, and if it had been Gideon who had put the call divert on her home phone number and an embargo on her calls at work, she'd have been immensely grateful, but for David to do it…

'You just don't get it, do you?' she exclaimed. 'You really can't see why I don't want your help?'

'Too damn right I can't,' he said. 'Dammit, Rachel, we're friends.'

'You keep saying that, but we're not,' she said, driven beyond endurance. 'We were lovers six years ago—'

'I thought we were both,' he said, his eyes catching and holding hers. 'Lovers and friends, and that's what I'd very much like us to be again.'

She would, too, if she thought there was any future in it, but there wasn't.

'No, David.'

'What do you want, Rachel? The moon, the stars? I'll get them for you.'

She didn't want the moon and the stars. She wanted him to love her—really love her—and she shook her head. 'Never go back—that's what people say, and they're right.'

'There's also a song about love being better the second time around.'

Her lip curled slightly. 'That particular song's about love, David, not sex.'

'Same thing,' he said dismissively, and she wondered how he could be so stupid. Gorgeous and desirable, but still stupid.

'No, they are not the same thing,' she retorted, 'and maybe when you finally grow up you might realise it.'

He stared at her thoughtfully for a second, then a warm, wide smile spread across his face. 'You know something? You really are very, very cute when you're mad.'

She glared at him, but the more she glared the more he smiled, and eventually she couldn't help herself. She burst out laughing. 'Oh, David, you are *impossible*!'

'But you love me?'

She did. 'Not enough to get involved with you again.'

'We'll see.'

'Anyone ever tell you arrogance isn't a very attractive quality in a man?' she observed, getting riled all over again because he was so damn sure of her, and she knew that she still wanted him.

'I'm not arrogant,' he said. 'I just know what you want.'

He didn't. He might think that he did, but he didn't.

'I have to go,' she said.

'What about your coffee and sandwiches?'

'They'll keep.'

'Like Saturday.' His blue eyes gleamed. 'Unfinished business, right?'

'Not in your lifetime,' she said, and made good her escape before she did something really dumb like agreeing with him.

'Are you OK?' Annie said, emerging so fast from the office that it was clear she'd been waiting. 'It sounded pretty fearsome in there.'

'I'm fine,' Rachel insisted. 'As for your brother...' She

shook her head and laughed. 'It would take a sledgehammer to dent his self-confidence.'

Annie managed a small smile in return, but her smile faded when Rachel walked away, and it had completely gone when she opened the staffroom door.

'Where'd you get to?' her brother asked as soon as he saw her. 'One minute you were there, gasping for a coffee, and the next you were gone. Sit down, put your feet up and I'll make you a coffee.' He switched on the kettle and picked up a cup. 'Do you want ordinary or decaffeinated?'

'What I want is some answers.'

He glanced over his shoulder to see his sister gazing at him with an expression he'd never seen before, and frowned. 'Answers to what?'

'David, I know your private life is your own—'

'Glad you realise that.'

'But what you're doing with Rachel is wrong. I don't know what happened after you took her home from the ball—'

'Nothing happened.'

'And I don't want to know, but I want you to stop what you're doing right now.'

'Annie, *nothing happened*.'

'So Rachel had second thoughts, did she?' his sister said shrewdly. 'Sensible girl, but you're not going to leave it at that, are you? Ever since you met up with her again, you've been making a play for her, and I want you to stop.'

A smile touched his lips. 'It's always the same when a woman becomes pregnant. Her hormones go into overdrive, she starts getting flaky ideas—'

'David, I *like* Rachel. I never thought I'd hear myself say that, but I do, and she doesn't deserve to be messed about by you.'

He lifted his own cup of coffee and drained it. 'Is that what you think I'm doing?'

'You want me to tell you what I think?' Annie demanded. 'OK, I'll tell you what I think. I think you were furious with Rachel when she left you. Not hurt, not upset, but furious. If you'd dumped her as you've dumped every other girl you've gone out with, everything would have been all right, but because she dumped you, it hurt your male pride, and now you've decided to try to win her back again so you can walk away this time.'

He banged his cup down on the worktop beside him with such force that his sister jumped, and when he spoke his voice was tight with ill-suppressed anger. 'First and foremost, I do *not* dump women. In fact—apart from Rachel—I've managed to remain very good friends with every woman I've ever dated.'

'Oh, really?' his sister said, matching him glare for glare. 'Send them all Christmas cards each year, do you—meet up with them for drinks occasionally?'

He coloured slightly. 'OK, so perhaps I don't exactly keep in touch with them…'

'I didn't think you did.'

'Knock it off, Annie.'

'No, I won't,' she exclaimed. 'David, if I thought for one minute that you'd fallen in love with Rachel I'd wish you all the luck in the world, but you haven't, have you?'

He threw her one of his best placating smiles. 'You know me, Annie.'

'I do, and that's why I want you to back off and leave her alone. I mean it, David,' his sister insisted as he tried to interrupt. 'Rachel deserves better than a three- or four-month fling with you.'

'And you're making too much of this,' he protested. 'Getting yourself worked up over nothing.'

'Am I?' She strode towards the staffroom door and opened it. 'I don't think I am, David, and I think if you were honest with yourself you'd admit that I'm right. If you can't do that…' she shook her head '…then you're not the man I thought you were.'

She was gone before he could reply, and for a second he stood motionless in the centre of the staffroom until he suddenly realised the kettle was boiling and with a muttered oath stretched to switch it off.

What the hell had got into his sister? It wasn't like her to interfere in his private life, and she'd got it all wrong—got him all wrong.

He'd never pursue a woman simply for revenge. Hell's bells, what kind of person would that make him? Somebody cold, and calculating, and shallow, and he was none of those things.

It was her hormones talking, that was all that it was, and he tried to laugh, but found that he couldn't. Instead, he stood in the staffroom, and the longer he stood the more troubled his expression became.

CHAPTER SEVEN

'I've had no problems at all with the Clomid, Dr Dunwoody,' Sable Mitchell declared brightly. 'I'm not pregnant yet, of course, but as I've only been on it a month I didn't expect to be.'

'So there's nothing you'd like to discuss with me?' Rachel said, glancing across at Sable's husband whose expression was tight.

'Not really, no,' the woman replied. 'In fact, all I need is another prescription.'

She needed something else, too, Rachel thought, sitting back in her seat with a frown. Sable might be happy, but her husband most clearly was anything but.

'What about you, Mr Mitchell?' she said. 'Is there anything you'd like to ask?'

Sable shot her husband one of those wifely say-a-word-and-you're-dead-meat looks, and he muttered, 'No.' Then he sat up straighter in his seat, his jaw firm. 'Yes, dammit, there is.'

'Donald—'

'I know I promised I wouldn't say anything, Sable,' he exclaimed, 'but I can't sit here and listen to you lying to the doctor. You're not fine on the Clomid. In fact, ever since you started it you've been wretched. Throwing up all the time—'

'Twice. I've been sick twice—'

'Bleeding constantly—'

'The doctor said that would happen,' Sable protested, her colour high. 'She said I'd have irregular bleeding—'

'Not that you'd become virtually housebound because of it,' Donald retorted, then shook his head as his wife

115

glared at him. 'Look, love, I want a baby as much as you do, but that damned pill is making you ill, and no baby is worth you feeling so awful.'

'I'm not going to stop taking the drug,' Sable said defiantly. 'OK, so I might have been bleeding rather more than I'd expected, but—'

'Sable, you're going through a packet of sanitary towels a day.'

'It's my body.'

'OK, let's take a deep breath here and try to talk about this calmly,' Rachel interrupted as the husband and wife squared up, clearly set to do battle. 'Sable, Clomid might have some side-effects, but what you're experiencing isn't acceptable. No, let me finish,' she added as the woman tried to interrupt. 'As we told you when we saw you last month, Clomid isn't the only infertility drug. There are others we can try—tamoxifen and Cyclofenil, to name but two.

'Then…then you're not going to tell me you won't treat me any more?' Sable said, and Rachel smiled.

'Of course I'm not. Just because this treatment has disagreed with you doesn't mean we're throwing in the towel.'

'I thought…' Sable bit her lip. 'I thought if I told you what was happening, you wouldn't let me come back. That I'd have to accept I wasn't going to have a baby.'

'All that's happened is this particular drug doesn't agree with you,' Rachel said gently. 'Infertility treatment isn't an exact science, Sable. What might suit you won't suit another woman, and vice versa. It's pretty much trial and error at the start, and your husband was right to tell me you were having problems.'

Donald Mitchell threw his wife a look which spoke volumes, and leant forward in his seat. 'This tamoxifen you're talking about, Doctor. Does Sable take it the same way as she took the Clomid?'

Rachel nodded as she reached for her prescription pad.

'It's a pill just like Clomid, and she'll have to take one every day for the five days preceding her period. I'm giving you a prescription for two months' supply,' she continued as she held out the prescription to Sable, 'but I'll also make you an appointment to see us again next month in case the tamoxifen doesn't agree with you.'

'Could you make it a morning appointment again?' Donald asked when he and his wife got to their feet. 'I work afternoon shifts, you see, and with a morning appointment it means I don't have to take time off work.'

'No problem,' Rachel replied, making a note in her appointment book.

'Will I see you when I come in for my next appointment?' Sable asked, and Rachel smiled.

'Unless you'd prefer to see Mr Hart?'

Sable shook her head firmly. 'Mr Hart's very nice, but… You're a woman, Doctor, and it's somehow much easier, talking to a woman.'

But not any easier to tell me the truth, Rachel thought wryly as she accompanied the couple to the door.

'If you find that you're bleeding as badly on the tamoxifen as you did on the Clomid, don't wait until your next appointment to tell us,' she said. 'Just ring our receptionist, and we'll squeeze you in somewhere.'

Sable nodded. 'Thanks for being so understanding, Doctor. I know it was stupid not to say anything, but—'

'You'd put up with any amount of discomfort to have a baby,' Rachel finished for her with a smile. 'I know, but don't do it again, OK?'

'I won't.' Sable laughed, then she looked up at Rachel a little shyly. 'You know, it's odd, Doctor, but when I saw you in Obstetrics and Gynaecology with Mr Caldwell, I thought you were a bit…well, a bit remote, but it shows how wrong you can be about a person, doesn't it?'

Rachel managed to keep on smiling until the Mitchells had left, but only just. It had been bad enough when she'd discovered her colleagues had thought she was cold and remote, but to learn that her patients had thought so, too…

How had she managed to become so distant without realising it? When she'd been a junior doctor she'd certainly vowed that if she ever became a specialist registrar her ward would never be as sloppily run as some she'd worked on, but she'd never imagined that her drive for efficiency would have been at the expense of her own humanity.

Her lips twisted slightly as she walked back to her desk and put her appointment book into the top drawer. To think she had David of all people to thank for opening her eyes. If he hadn't come back into her life, and Annie hadn't been his sister, she would never have known what she'd become.

'Rachel, have you a minute?'

Annie was hovering indecisively in her consulting-room doorway, and Rachel straightened up with an effort. 'Of course. What's up?'

'It's those post-coital samples I took for you last Thursday. The results still aren't back from the lab. I've phoned them a dozen times but they're giving me the runaround so…'

'You'd like me to rattle their cage?' Rachel smiled. 'No problem. Rattling people's cages is my speciality.'

'I used to be able to do it,' Annie said ruefully. 'If people were giving me the runaround I used to be able to kick ass if I needed to, but lately…' She shook her head. 'If anybody looks at me sideways I just want to burst into tears.'

'It's because you're pregnant,' Rachel said gently. 'Your hormones are all over the place.'

'No, it's more than that, it's…' Annie bit her lip. 'I think perhaps Gideon was right, and I'm doing too much.'

Rachel's heart sank as she stared at Annie. She had a horrible suspicion she knew what was coming next, and the thought filled her with dismay. Annie had been such a help since they'd opened the clinic—performing all their blood and urine tests, checking progesterone and oestrogen levels—and if she handed in her notice…

'You're thinking of resigning, aren't you?' she said, hoping she was wrong but guessing she wasn't.

'I'm so tired all the time, Rachel,' Annie said awkwardly. 'I'm just fifteen weeks pregnant, yet I feel like I'm on my last trimester. I've no energy, no oomph…'

'Then you must hand in your notice right away,' Rachel declared with a firmness she was very far from feeling.

'But how will you and David manage?' Annie protested. 'The unit's hardly overstaffed, even with me helping you, and David still hasn't arranged any interviews for his permanent members of staff.'

'He'll just have to get off his butt and arrange them,' Rachel said. 'The important thing here is you and your baby, and we'll manage.' She didn't know quite how, but they were going to have to. 'How much notice do you have to give?' she asked as she followed Annie out of her room and into the corridor.

'A month.'

'Then I suggest you go up to Admin and do it now.'

'But—'

'Just do it, Annie,' Rachel insisted. 'David and I—' She came to a halt. He was crossing the hall at the end of the corridor and as she watched him disappear into his room she didn't realise her face had softened, but Annie saw it.

'You're still stuck on him, aren't you?' she said with resignation, and hot colour flooded Rachel's cheeks.

'No, I'm not. Well, OK, maybe I am, just a little,' she admitted as Annie shook her head. 'But—'

'Rachel, he's my brother, and I love him to bits but, please, don't get involved with him again. You know what he's like.'

Rachel did, just as she also knew that she was in love with him, and always would be. 'Annie—'

'What he's offering you—there's no future in it. A two-

or three-month fling at the most, and then he'll be off with somebody else.'

Yes, but at least I'd have those two or three months, Rachel thought wistfully, instead of a lifetime of wondering and wishing. OK, so maybe she'd told him on Saturday night that she'd settle for nothing less than full commitment, but settling for just three months was suddenly beginning to sound pretty darned good.

'He'll hurt you, Rachel,' Annie continued doggedly. 'Is that what you want—to be hurt again?'

Of course she didn't. No woman in her right mind would want to be hurt, but staying in your right mind when somebody like David Hart was smiling at you, teasing you, telling you he would give you the stars and the moon, wasn't easy.

'Rachel, think about this,' Annie said persuasively, clearly reading her mind. 'Remember why you left him in the first place.'

Because I couldn't handle the uncertainty, she remembered. Because I didn't want to be just another name in his little address book.

Yes, but it would be different this time, she told herself. This time I'd know what I was letting myself in for. This time I'd have no illusions, no unrealistic hopes, and I'm older...

But no wiser, her heart jeered, and she shut it up quickly.

'Annie—'

'Don't break your heart for a dream, Rachel. And that's what will happen if you go down that road.'

'Annie—'

'Sorry to interrupt, Doctors,' Pam said, appearing beside them without warning, 'but I've some requisition forms Rachel needs to sign.'

Normally Rachel would have groaned, but not today. Today she was only too relieved to have an excuse to escape. Annie clearly meant well, but she didn't need somebody telling her she was an idiot. She already suspected that she was.

Nor did she need any more complications in her life, she thought after she'd signed Pam's forms and made an appointment for Sable Mitchell to see her in a month's time, only to realise that the receptionist was very quiet. And not just quiet but looking as miserable as Annie had earlier, with suspiciously bright eyes.

Surely—oh, surely—she wasn't planning on leaving, too? Annie handing in her resignation was going to make life difficult enough, but if Pam was thinking of throwing in the towel as well...

'Everything OK, Pam?' she asked hopefully, and to her dismay the receptionist gave a very decided sniff.

'No, it's not. I'm sorry, Rachel, but I don't see how he can blame me when I told him about it weeks ago. I told him that organising these things took time. I said he should get the wheels started, and now he says it's my fault, and he wants it done in double-quick time, and I don't see how I can.'

Rachel stared blankly at the receptionist, then shook her head. 'I'm sorry, but you're going to have to back up here and start again. Who did you tell what, and how is it your fault?'

Pam dug a handkerchief out of her pocket and blew her nose. 'Mr Hart. I told him the day after the unit opened that Admin were anxious for him to appoint his permanent staff as quickly as possible. I said there'd been quite a few applications, but I couldn't start arranging any interviews until he'd given me his timetable.'

'Sounds reasonable to me.' Rachel nodded.

'I kept asking and asking for the timetable, and he kept saying there was no hurry, and now this morning he suddenly comes into the office and says he wants to start interviewing next week. I told him it wasn't possible—that I still didn't have his timetable—and he...and he...'

'He gave you a rocket?' Rachel exclaimed, anger rising in her as a tear rolled down the receptionist's cheek.

'Not a rocket, no, but he *looked* at me, Doctor. You know how some men don't actually have to say anything yet you can tell by their look that they think you're an idiot?'

Rachel did. Greg would have won prizes for his looks. She'd never seen David use any, but maybe he'd been keeping them in reserve, or maybe...

'I think this could be my fault,' she murmured awkwardly. 'You see, I was chivvying him yesterday about the interviews—pointing out that I'm supposed to be returning to Obs and Gynae at the beginning of September—and it looks like I've actually got through to him, and now he's panicking.'

'Well, fine,' Pam sniffed, 'but there was no need for him to take it out on me.'

'I'll have a word with him,' Rachel said. 'Have you a blank timetable I can wave under his nose?'

The receptionist pulled open a drawer in her filing cabinet. 'I need to know the dates and times of every operation he has planned for the next four weeks and what consultations he's arranged. There's no point in me setting up interviews, only to have him dash off in the middle of them.'

'Absolutely,' Rachel agreed. 'And don't take what happened too much to heart,' she continued as the receptionist blew her nose again. 'He probably just got out of the wrong side of the bed this morning.'

Most definitely the wrong side, she decided when she walked into David's room to be greeted by a deep frown.

'Something you want?' he said.

'And hello and good morning to you, too.' She smiled, but to her surprise he didn't smile back. Neither did he ask her to sit down, which was unusual, but she'd told Pam she was going to speak to him, and speak to him she would. 'I need to talk to you.'

'I'm rather busy at the moment.'

'Too busy, it seems, to remember that Pam has been asking for your timetable for weeks so she could set up your interviews,' she said, leaning back against the door, and folding her arms. 'But not too busy to come the heavy big boss when you discover nothing's been done.'

He flipped open the file on his desk and stared at it. 'So she's been complaining about me, has she?'

'Not complaining, no, but she's upset.' And look at me, dammit, when I'm talking to you, she thought with irritation. 'Every time she mentioned the interviews you said there was no hurry—'

'I've changed my mind.'

'And she's supposed to know that? David, she may be an excellent receptionist, but she doesn't have ESP, and to reduce her to tears—'

'She's crying?'

She'd got his attention at last, but he still wasn't looking at her. Which was weird. Yesterday he'd been full of compliments, saying he wanted them to become lovers again. Yesterday he'd even said he'd get her the moon and the stars if she wanted, and yet this morning she had the oddest feeling he just wanted her to go away.

'Of course she was crying,' she said, dragging her mind back to their receptionist with difficulty. 'I'd be crying, too, if somebody told me I was useless.'

'I never said she was useless.'

'You might not have actually said it, but that's how you've made her feel.'

He muttered something that sounded suspiciously like 'Women!' under his breath, but before she could call him on it, he'd got to his feet.

'I'll speak to her. Now, if there's nothing else…?'

What the hell was going on? she wondered as he walked over to his filing cabinet, yanked open a drawer with rather more force than was necessary and thrust the file he'd been reading into it. OK, so yesterday she'd told him she wasn't going to get involved with him again, but he'd said he was going to change her mind. Not that she had any intention of letting him change her mind. Well, maybe she had sort of considered it, vaguely. Vaguely? Hell, she'd done nothing but think about it since last night, and now he was blanking her.

'David…' She took a step towards him, only to see him take a step back. Dammit, she didn't bite, neither was she aware of having a personal hygiene problem, so what was happening here? 'David—'

'I have to go,' he said quickly. 'I'm due in Theatre at twelve-thirty, and I don't want to be late and cut into Mr Portman's time.'

He'd never given a damn about cutting into Andrew Portman's time before. In fact, she'd seen him deliberately arrive late for an operation just so he could overrun and wind up the overly slow orthopaedic surgeon.

'David—' He was already walking out of his room, and Rachel hurried after him. 'Look, what's going on?' There, she'd said it. Oh, Lord, he looked so uncomfortable and embarrassed, as though he wanted to be anywhere but here. 'I mean…I meant…'

He glanced at his watch. 'I'm sorry, but I really do have to go.'

He wanted to get away from her. The man who would have made love to her on Saturday night if she hadn't come to her senses wanted to get away from her, and there was only one possible explanation for his change of heart.

He'd decided she wasn't worth the effort. He'd thought about what she'd said to him and had decided she simply wasn't worth the effort.

Well, fine. She could live with that. If he wasn't interested in her any more, she was pleased, relieved. No, she wasn't. She felt stupidly hurt, as well as confused, and that only made her angrier.

'I'll leave you to it, then,' she said tightly.

'Rachel…'

He looked as unhappy as she felt. No, he didn't, she thought, disgusted with herself. He looked exactly as he always looked. Handsome and charming, and she was the village idiot.

'I think that's my phone ringing,' she lied.

'I didn't hear anything,' he said.

'Believe me, my phone's ringing,' she said more forcefully, and before he could reply she'd marched quickly down the corridor and into her room, banging the door shut behind her.

Slamming it shut would have been a more accurate description, he thought, raking his fingers through his hair with a groan, and it was all Annie's fault. Yesterday his life had been so simple. All he'd wanted had been Rachel back in his bed, naked and willing beneath him, gasping and arching as he plunged into her dark, wet sweetness, and then Annie had gone and said what she had and everything had changed.

He'd tried to forget her accusation. All yesterday afternoon he'd tried to wipe it from his mind, but it had refused to go away. It had kept on niggling and niggling at him until he'd given up and faced it, and to his dismay he'd been forced to acknowledge that his sister's words had held an unpalatable kernel of truth.

She'd been wrong when she'd said he wanted Rachel back for revenge. Anger might have been his first reaction when he'd met her again—an anger left over from York when she'd disappeared without a word, leaving him feeling like a fool—but the more he'd been in her company the more he'd wanted her for herself.

But not permanently. Annie had been right about that. Some men were the settling-down sort, some men weren't, and he most definitely wasn't.

'Could you sign for this for me, please, Mr Hart?'

He jerked round guiltily to see a lab technician holding out an envelope to him, and frowned. 'What is it?'

'Post-coital results for Dr Dunwoody. Normally I'd

hand them in to the office, but I'm running late, and...'
The technician smiled a little shamefacedly. 'The thing is,
they should have been completed last week, and you know
what women are like when they're in a temper.'

Do I ever, David thought grimly as he scrawled his
name on the receipt and the technician hurried gratefully
away.

If only his sister had kept her thoughts and her opinions
to herself. If only Rachel didn't want commitment.
Dammit, they'd had fun in York. They'd had a lot of fun
in York, so why couldn't she just be happy to go back to
the way they were?

All her talk about wanting stability in her life, a partner
and a baby. Why the hell would he want a baby or stability? Right now he could go where he liked, do what he
liked, and to give that all up...

Not even for Rachel was he prepared to give that all up,
which meant he had to back off from her from now on.
To continue pursuing her would make him the low-life,
shallow, calculating jerk his sister clearly thought he was,
so he had to back off, and last night it had sounded so
simple, so easy, but now...

'Was that the lab technician?'

Pam's head had appeared round her office door, and he
nodded. 'You've just missed him.'

'You mean the little worm skipped off before I could
speak to him,' she said wrathfully. 'He knew damn well
he'd get an earful from me for being so late with Rachel's
results.'

He smiled, but as the receptionist began to withdraw he
held out his hand to stay her. 'I owe you an apology, don't
I? It was very wrong of me to imply it was your fault the
interviews haven't been set up yet. I'll get my timetable
filled in today, and if you could try and get the interviews
organised for me as quickly as possible, I'd be immensely
grateful.'

Pam looked startled, then nodded awkwardly. 'I'll do my

best, Mr Hart, and there's no need to apologise. We all have our bad days.'

Some more than most, he thought grimly as he strode out of the Mackenzie unit, and this was going to be the first of many bad days for him until he could appoint Rachel's permanent replacement. Last night everything might have seemed easy, but when he'd seen her again this morning, looking so hurt and confused... His head might tell him that backing off from her was the correct and honourable thing to do, but his body didn't agree with the idea at all.

'You're a bit early for your laparoscopy, Mr Hart,' Sharon, the theatre sister, said in surprise when he arrived outside Theatre 2. 'Barry hasn't arrived to anaesthetise your twelve-thirty patient yet.'

'My watch must be fast,' he lied. 'Who's operating at the moment?'

'Lawrence Summers had the slot before you, but he's just finished.'

David groaned inwardly. If there was one surgeon he loathed more than old man Portman, it was the consultant in charge of Men's Surgical.

'No chance of me avoiding him, I suppose?' he asked, and the theatre sister chuckled.

'You shouldn't be stuck with him too long. He and his anaesthetist and three juniors went into the changing room about ten minutes ago.'

'*Three* juniors? What on earth was he performing this morning—open-heart surgery?'

'A duodenal, but Lawrence would need an audience if he was removing an ingrowing toenail.' A burst of male laughter came from the changing room, and Sharon shook her head. 'Honestly, I swear if that man was made of chocolate he'd eat himself.'

'He does have a rather high opinion of himself, doesn't he?' David grinned, and the theatre sister rolled her eyes.

'God's gift to the world is our Lawrence, though his

ego's taken a bit of a dent since Woody turned him down yesterday.'

David's eyebrows snapped together. 'He asked her out?'

'That's what I heard. I also heard she sent him away with a flea in his ear.'

It was just as well she had, David thought grimly when Sharon hurried away in answer to one of her staff's call. Lawrence Summers and Rachel? Over his dead body.

'Oops, am I late this morning, or are you early?' Barry asked, coming to an abrupt halt as he pushed open the swing doors.

'I'm early,' David muttered. 'Faulty watch.'

Another rumble of laughter came from the changing room, and Barry grimaced. 'Sounds like Lawrence is in fine form this morning.'

'Frankly I'm surprised he can still get his head through the doors,' David declared, but as he and the anaesthetist walked towards the changing room it gradually became all too disastrously clear that the consultant in charge of Men's Surgical wasn't talking about his surgical prowess as usual, but about Rachel.

'David, ignore it,' Barry said quickly as the words 'tease' and 'she was obviously asking for it' drifted out to them. 'You know what Lawrence is like.'

'Too damned right I do,' David said angrily, 'and he's not going to talk about Rachel like that.'

'David, wait—'

But he didn't wait. He pushed past the anaesthetist and into the changing room, and Lawrence Summers's juniors took one look at his face and scuttled towards the sinks.

'Well, look who's here,' the consultant declared, completely unperturbed. 'It's the lovely Rachel's boss. Maybe he can tell us more about the hitherto unsuspected talents she displayed so enticingly on Saturday.'

'What I can tell you, Summers, is that I do not take kindly to you discussing a member of my staff who's not here to defend herself,' David said tightly.

'What's there to defend?' the consultant countered. 'Any woman who wears a dress like the one Woody wore on Saturday is saying only one thing. "I'm available".'

'David, leave it,' Barry warned as David's lips set into a thin white line of anger, but there was no way he was going to. He knew men talked about women—their faces, their figures, their availability. Hell, he'd done it himself in the past, but this was different. This was Rachel.

'I wouldn't suggest you try using that argument as a defence in a court of law,' David snapped. 'And personally I think a woman should be able to wear whatever she likes without a group of men with the mindsets of a lot of sniggering schoolboys calling her morals or intentions into question. Rachel Dunwoody happens to be a friend of mine—'

'Oh, really?' Lawrence sneered. 'Enough of a friend for you to be able to tell us whether the charms we all saw on Saturday are real, or the results of recent clever surgery?'

David took a step forward, his hands clenched into tight fists, his face dark with anger. 'Summers, if you don't shut your mouth right now you'll be eating your meals through a straw for the next few weeks.'

The consultant's eyebrows rose. 'Overreacting a bit, aren't we, Hart? After all, I'm only saying what everybody else is. That the dress she wore on Saturday was an invitation, and any woman who doesn't deliver after sending out such blatant signals of availability, is no more than a prick tease.'

'David!'

The anaesthetist was too late. Before he could catch hold of David's arm to restrain him, he'd lunged across the room and slammed the consultant from Men's Surgical hard up against the wall.

'Now, listen to me, Summers, and listen good,' he ground out. 'One more word—just one more…'

'What's wrong, Hart?' Lawrence Summers gasped. 'Didn't she put out for you either?'

'Lawrence, for God's sake, shut up,' Barry exclaimed. 'And, David, are you out of your mind? Remember who you are—your career...'

'Tell that to this foul-mouthed jerk,' David retorted. 'He's the one with a mind like a sewer.'

'A mind like a sewer, have I?' Lawrence wheezed. 'What about you? You're not asking me to believe you weren't turned on when you saw her in that dress.'

He had been, David thought as he stared at the consultant in horror. Oh, Lord, but he had. When she'd opened her front door that night, all he'd wanted had been to drag her down to the floor and make love to her.

But he hadn't. That was the important thing, he told himself. OK, so he'd thought he'd go crazy at the ball, seeing her dance by in the arms of other men, and when they'd gone back to her house and she'd let him touch her, he'd thought he'd been about to explode, but he would never have forced himself on her. When she'd told him to go, he'd gone. His body may have felt frustrated because it hadn't got what it wanted, but what he'd most felt had been...

Intrigued, he realised with dismay. Intrigued because she'd turned him down flat. Intrigued because she'd suddenly seemed even more of a challenge, which meant he was as arrogant and as full of his own conceit as Lawrence Summers.

'That's more like it,' Barry declared with relief as David's grip on Lawrence loosened. 'You're both intelligent, professional men, and to be behaving like—'

'Overgrown schoolboys?' Lawrence suggested, smoothing down the creases in the lapels of his pinstriped suit with a smile that made David long to make good his threat about the straw. 'I agree with you, so why don't we shake hands, Hart, and agree Woody's not worth it?'

David stared at the consultant's outstretched hand, then

met his eyes coldly. 'Her name is Rachel, and you're encroaching on my theatre time.'

The consultant gazed back at him for a moment, then shrugged.

'Suit yourself,' he said, and with a perfunctory nod towards Barry he beckoned to his anaesthetist and junior doctors and strolled out of the changing room.

'That was…unpleasant,' Barry murmured, mopping his forehead with his handkerchief.

'That's one way of putting it,' David declared, and the anaesthetist glanced at him awkwardly.

'I know you were angry, but— OK, OK, I won't say any more,' the anaesthetist continued as he encountered a look which had him stepping back a pace. 'All I will say is thank the Lord you came to your senses and didn't actually hit him. Lawrence… He can be a vindictive bastard when he wants, and if he'd filed a complaint about you with Admin…'

It would have finished his career, David realised as Barry lifted a set of theatre scrubs from the shelf and disappeared into one of the cubicles, but it had never occurred to him. Not once had the possible consequences of his actions occurred to him. All he'd wanted had been to shut the consultant up and protect Rachel.

Careful, his mind whispered. Wanting to protect a woman, to stop her from being hurt—that's coming pretty close to involvement, commitment.

Rubbish, he argued back. He'd only done what any right-thinking man would have done in the circumstances.

Really? His mind laughed, and he shook his head vehemently. One thing was certain. The sooner he got those interviews organised, and Rachel's replacement appointed, the better it was going to be for everybody.

CHAPTER EIGHT

'THE secret of success in this op is to take as small a slice as possible from each ovary,' David declared as Rachel reached for a scalpel. 'You're not attempting to reshape them, simply to remove the tiniest sliver.'

'I still don't see how it works,' she said. 'I mean, how can taking a small piece out of each of a woman's ovaries kick-start her ovulation?'

'I don't know, and neither did Dr Stein and Dr Leventhal who discovered the treatment,' he replied. 'In fact, they were amazed to find that women who had stopped ovulating suddenly started again after they'd removed small samples from their ovaries for testing. Perhaps it somehow prevents the overproduction of hormones, but frankly your guess is as good as mine.'

Rachel didn't have a guess. She was too busy wondering how he could have the nerve to smile at her, and he was smiling. She might only be able to see his blue eyes above his surgical mask but those eyes were twinkling, and if he thought he could get round her that easily after the stunt he'd pulled in the changing rooms last week, then he didn't know her. Which he didn't.

'If this op doesn't work, there's nothing else you can do for Mrs Taylor, is there?' Sharon said, moving the trolley of sterilised instruments closer to Rachel.

'There isn't, no,' David said before Rachel could reply. 'But complete ovarian failure is an odd disorder. For some reason a woman's ovaries can just go to sleep, then wake up again for no apparent reason.'

'They're going to have to wake up pretty damn fast in this case,' Rachel said dryly as she carefully removed a piece of the right ovary. 'Mrs Taylor will be thirty-nine next month.'

'Didn't *The Lancet* have an article last month about a woman with complete ovarian failure becoming pregnant for the first time at forty-two?' Barry said, adjusting the dials of his monitors.

'I'm afraid the fact that her case made it into *The Lancet* shows how very rare it is,' David replied. 'Something wrong?' he continued, seeing Rachel frown.

'I'm just trying to decide whether I've taken out enough,' she said.

David moved closer to her and squinted over her shoulder. 'Looks fine to me. If you take the same amount from her left ovary, that should be perfect.'

'Right.'

'The main thing to remember is not to take out too much tissue.'

'So you said,' she murmured, all too uncomfortably aware of his closeness and furious with herself because she was so aware of it. 'Look, could you give me some elbow room here?' she continued more sharply than she'd intended, and heard him mutter a disjointed apology as he stepped back.

Well, good, she thought waspishly as she selected a fresh scalpel from the instrument trolley. Why the hell should she be the only one feeling harassed and persecuted, especially as she was the innocent party in this whole damn shambles.

'BP normal, pulse rate fine, heart rate A-OK,' Barry declared. 'I hear one of the technicians from Haematology saw Liz and Sandy Fenton coming out of the cinema together last night, so it's official. They really are dating.'

Sharon rolled her eyes heavenwards. 'I still can't believe it. I mean, no offence to the poor bloke, but what in the world does Liz see in him? All he ever talks about is bladder diseases.'

'And Rhode Island Reds.' Barry grinned. 'Don't forget his Rhode Island Reds.'

'What's a Rhode Island Red?' David asked curiously, and Rachel murmured, 'It's a chicken,' as she began removing a slice from the left ovary.

'He must have bored her into going out with him,' Sharon declared, quickly moving the trolley of sterilised instruments sideways as Rachel altered her position to get a better look at what she was doing. 'It's the only possible explanation. He must have talked and talked about his damn bladder diseases and chickens, and Liz must have said yes just to shut him up.'

'Now, that's what I call a novel approach.' Barry laughed. 'Boring a girl into submission. Maybe I should give it a try some time.'

'I suppose it couldn't be any worse than some of the feeble, cringe-making chat-up lines you men come up with,' Sharon exclaimed. 'Do you remember when Lawrence Summers—'

The theatre sister came to a scarlet-cheeked halt, but she was too late, the damage had already been done. The relaxed atmosphere in the operating theatre had disappeared in an instant, and Rachel bit her lip behind her theatre mask.

A week. It had been a week now since David and Lawrence Summers had—depending upon whose version of events you believed—either almost come to blows in the changing room or actually had come to blows, and still people were talking about it.

Talking about her. Not about Lawrence, or David, but about her. The exact sequence of events might be hazy, but the one thing everybody was in agreement about was that the argument had been about her.

What the hell had got into him? OK, so Lawrence appeared to have said something derogatory about her, and she could pretty well guess what it had been, but David should have ignored it, not made her the subject of even more gossip that she already was because of That Dress.

'Do…do you want dissolvable sutures?' Sharon muttered, clearly wishing the ground would open up and swallow her.

It was on the tip of Rachel's tongue to retort that she'd hardly be wanting anything else for an internal operation, but the poor theatre sister looked so conscience-stricken that she quickly bit back her acid reply.

'Dissolvables are fine,' she said, and as the sister handed them to her she sensed David's eyes on her and deliberately refused to meet his gaze.

He hadn't even apologised to her for making her the talk of the hospital. He hadn't even told her what had actually happened. She'd had to hear about it from Gideon's receptionist and, boy, had the woman revelled in telling her the lurid details.

'I hear the head of Paediatrics is retiring,' Barry said brightly, far too brightly, and Sharon shot him a grateful look.

'I wonder who'll get his job?' she replied. 'The grapevine says it's going to be an internal promotion.'

'Which would make sense, but then again Admin might opt for bringing in fresh blood,' the anaesthetist continued, as though it was the most riveting subject in the world. And as he and Sharon went on to discuss the relevant merits of the various members of Paediatrics, Rachel kept her head down and wished she was sticking the scalpel she was using into David.

'How does the left ovary look?' he murmured.

'Fine,' she replied tightly.

'Would you like me to suture for you?'

'Only if you don't think I can do it properly myself,' she muttered, but he heard her. She knew from his sharp intake of breath that he'd heard her, but what did he expect?

High-handed, that was what he was. High-handed, officious and interfering. He'd been exactly the same with Greg, ignoring all her protestations that she could deal with it herself, pushing himself in where he wasn't wanted. OK, so she was grateful not to have received any more phone calls, but that wasn't the point. The point was she was almost thirty years old and she didn't need—or want—him meddling in things that didn't concern him.

'Try to keep the stitches as small as you can,' he said as she began suturing. 'The smaller the stitches are the less chance there is of any adhesions developing.'

'I know,' she replied, keeping her eyes fixed on what she was doing.

'If you keep your wrist at a right angle it will minimise the pull on the tissue.'

'I *know*, and I need to concentrate, OK?' she exclaimed, and felt rather than saw Barry and Sharon exchange glances.

Oh, terrific, Rachel. Now everybody would have even more to talk about, but she didn't care. She'd had enough, and all she wanted was to get the operation over and herself as far away from David as she could.

It was easier said than done. Even when Sharon and Barry had wheeled Mrs Taylor into the recovery room, there was still the changing room to negotiate, and David seemed in no hurry to put on a fresh set of scrubs for his next operation.

'You did an excellent job in there,' he commented. 'In fact, we should be able to discharge Mrs Taylor in a few days.'

'Good,' she said, pulling off her theatre cap. 'Now, if you'll excuse me—'

'You're sure you can't stay to assist me with the endometriosis op?'

Luckily, she couldn't. 'I have a consultation in twenty minutes.'

'It's just that it would have been good practice for you—'

'Only if I was planning on becoming an infertility specialist, which I'm not.'

He stared down at his hands for a second, then straightened up. 'Right. Did Pam tell you she's managed to arrange the first of the interviews for a week on Friday?'

She hadn't, and Rachel was tempted to say it was amazing how fast he could get off his butt when he wanted to get rid of somebody, but she didn't.

'Right,' she said instead. 'Now, if you'll—'

'I'd like you to sit in with me when I do the interviews. You know how the clinic works,' he added as her eyebrows rose, 'and I'd appreciate a second opinion on the candidates.'

'I'm not sure if I'll be free that day.'

'I've made sure you are,' he replied, and saw her jaw tighten. 'Rachel—'

'You're the boss,' she said, throwing her cap towards the bin. But it missed, and as she stepped forward to retrieve it he did, too.

'With an aim like that you'll never get a job with the New York Yankees,' he said, picking up the cap and binning it.

'Just as well I'm not applying for one, then,' she replied, only to feel her pulse kick up when his lips curved into a smile.

She was hopeless, absolutely hopeless. This man had made her a laughing stock. This man wasn't interested in her, not even for a brief fling, and yet all he had to do was smile and she knew she was still stuck on him, still hopelessly in love with him, and she was an idiot.

'I have to go,' she muttered, but as she turned on her heel he put out his hand, not quite touching her.

'Rachel… Rachel, I'm sorry I've made you the subject of so much gossip and speculation.'

She wanted to say, So you should be, and you're a total jerk, but what she actually said was, 'It's OK.'

David shook his head. 'No, it's not. Ever since I met up

with you again I seem to have caused you nothing but trouble, and I swear I never meant to. I only wanted…'

Her breath caught in her throat as his voice trailed away into silence. He was gazing down at her almost as though he'd never truly seen her before. Gazing down at her with such heat in his deep blue eyes that her heart did a queer little back flip and she had to swallow, hard.

'You…you only wanted what?' she asked, hoping she didn't sound quite as breathless as she felt.

'Sorry?'

'You said… You said "I only wanted" and then you stopped.'

'Did I?'

She nodded, and ran her tongue nervously along her lips, and saw something deep and dark flare in his eyes.

'I can't remember,' he said huskily. 'Rachel…'

Had he taken a step forward? She hadn't noticed him taking a step forward but he seemed closer, felt closer. 'David—'

'Your three o'clock's arrived, Mr Hart,' Sharon declared, pushing open the door of the changing room with her elbow. 'She's had her pre-med, so do you want Barry to anaesthetise her or…?'

'Ask him to anaesthetise her for me.'

'Will do.'

Sharon disappeared, and Rachel cleared her throat.

'You were saying…?' she began hesitantly, and he yanked off his theatre cap and crushed it between his fingers.

'I just…' He shook his head, and to her surprise she saw a sudden flash of anger in his eyes. Not anger directed at her, she sensed, but anger that was for some strange reason levelled at himself. 'Look, I'm sorry about what happened, that's all. What I did with Lawrence… It was stupid. *I* was stupid.'

Stupid. He thought he'd been stupid to defend her. Stupid to take exception to what Lawrence had said, and she was dumb, dumb, dumb.

Even after all that had happened a part of her had hoped—dreamed—that he might actually one day grow to care for her, to love her, but he didn't care, and he wasn't the stupid one, she was. The stupid one who had even—heaven help her—actually considered having yet another brief affair with him.

'I have to go,' she said through a throat so tight it hurt.

'Rachel—'

'You've made your apology so everything's all right now, isn't it?' she said, and as she walked into one of the changing cubicles and firmly closed the door, he screwed the theatre cap he was holding into a small, tight ball.

She was right. Everything should have been fine now, but it wasn't. Not by a long shot.

Hell's teeth, what was the matter with him? He'd apologised to her. He'd been backing off from her as his sister had ordered, so why did he feel so depressed, and irritable, and confused?

In the past, when he'd walked away from a relationship, the only emotion he'd felt had been relief. Relief that he was free again. But with Rachel…

Dammit, they hadn't even had a relationship, not this time, so why was it proving so hard to distance himself from her? Heaven knew, he'd dated prettier girls in the past, girls with better figures…

None with such a cute butt, his mind pointed out, but cute butts weren't everything, and neither was thick auburn hair, or light grey eyes, or skin the colour and texture of white satin.

It didn't make any sense. The way he was feeling didn't make any sense. She was like an itch he didn't seem able to get rid of. An itch that had somehow got right under his skin.

'Ready whenever you are, Mr Hart,' Sharon said, sticking her head round the changing-room door, and he nodded.

Work. What he needed was work. If he could just keep himself busy until Rachel's replacement arrived then everything would be fine. When he couldn't see her every day, couldn't watch her face light up with laughter or hear her voice, then everything would be fine. He knew it would be.

'I think we're going to have a storm,' Pam said, glancing uneasily through her office window at the black clouds gathering overhead. 'And guess who hasn't even brought a coat with her today, far less an umbrella.'

'Snap.' Rachel smiled. 'I suppose the hot weather couldn't last, and we could do with something to clear the air.'

Pam didn't look convinced. 'Have you finished with those files?' she asked, reaching for the ones Rachel was holding.

'Not quite. I just want to check through them to make sure all the tests I suggested have been carried out. Is Annie around?'

'Last I saw her was on her way to take some blood samples from those three new patients you saw this afternoon.' The receptionist frowned slightly. 'Mind you, that was quite a while ago. Do you want me to see if I can find her?'

'If you could.' Rachel nodded. 'I want to make sure everything is in order before she leaves. I know she still has another three weeks to work, but I want to double-check all the samples she's taken to ensure there's no loose ends.'

'It's going to be strange without her, isn't it?' the receptionist said. 'Mind you, it's going to be strange without you, too.'

'I was only ever meant to be here temporarily,' Rachel said bracingly.

'Even so—'

'If you should see Annie, would you ask her to come to my room?' Rachel said quickly, and made good her escape before the receptionist could say anything else.

The trouble was that Pam was right, she thought with a sigh as she walked down the corridor to her consulting room. It was going to be strange, not working here any more. When Gideon had first suggested she help get the unit up and running, it had been the last thing she'd wanted to do, but now...

She opened the door of her room and stared at the buttercup yellow walls. How long had it been since she and David had painted them? Not even two months, and yet it seemed like a lifetime ago. There was so much she was going to miss about the Mackenzie unit. The patients she'd seen, all of them desperately holding onto a hope, a dream. All of them looking to her to fulfil those dreams. She could understand why David had switched specialities, and if things had been different...

Unconsciously she shook her head. Don't break your heart over a dream, Annie had said, and she'd been right. The only thing she could do was to apply for a job in an infertility unit somewhere else. There was nothing to keep her in Glasgow any more, and if she could just sell the house...

She groaned inwardly. She had more chance of becoming a size ten by next week. There was only a little over two weeks left until the deadline Greg had given her, but nobody had shown any real interest and—

'Hey, watch that paintwork,' she protested with a smile as Pam threw open the door of her consulting room with such force that it banged against the wall, scraping the emulsion. 'I'll have you know Mr Hart and I put in three days' hard slog on this unit—'

'Rachel, it's Annie. She's in the toilets, and she's bleeding.'

Rachel was on her feet and running before the receptionist had even finished. Down the corridor, around the corner and into the women's toilets, where she slewed to a halt, her heart twisting inside her as she saw Annie lying on the floor, blood seeping clearly through the skirt of her pale blue cotton dress.

'I didn't do anything stupid—honestly I didn't,' Annie gasped, trying to lever herself upright. 'I was just washing my hands, and I suddenly felt this awful pain and, oh, Rachel, make the bleeding stop. Please—please, make the bleeding stop.'

'Is she having a miscarriage?' Pam said breathlessly. 'Is she losing—?'

'Help me get Annie into my consulting room, then page Gideon and the lab and tell them we want a technician to work the ultrasound scanner up here immediately,' Rachel rapped out.

The receptionist did as she asked, but when Rachel had made Annie as comfortable as she could on her examination table, she said uncertainly, 'What about Mr Hart? Should I page him, too, or will he still be in the middle of an operation?'

Rachel tried to remember David's schedule but gave up. 'Just go and keep watch for the technician, Pam.'

The receptionist nodded, but as soon as she'd gone Annie clasped Rachel's hand, pain and fear plain on her face.

'Pam was right, wasn't she? I'm losing the baby, and it's all my fault. I didn't want it—not when I first found out I was pregnant. I thought it was too soon, that Gideon and I should wait, but now... It's a judgment on me, isn't it? A judgment on me for saying I didn't want it.'

'Of course it's not,' Rachel insisted. 'And we don't know if you're losing the baby. Lots of women bleed a little in the early weeks of pregnancy.'

But sixteen weeks wasn't early pregnancy, she thought as she packed sterilised wadding between Annie's legs, and Annie wasn't bleeding a little. It was coming from her in clots.

Dimly she heard the sound of running feet coming down the corridor, then the door banged open and Gideon stood there, his face pale, his breathing laboured. Annie took one look at his face and the tears she had been holding in check overflowed.

'Gideon, I'm sorry—so sorry. It's all my fault. You said I was doing too much—that I should give up work, and rest—but I wouldn't listen, and now… Oh, Gideon, I don't want to lose the baby. Please, oh, please—don't let me lose our baby.'

He clasped her hands tightly in his, then rounded on Rachel, panic and distress plain in his eyes. 'Where's the damned ultrasound technician? You have sent for one, haven't you?'

'He'll be here any minute,' Rachel said soothingly, and he was.

With a speed that was amazing the technician linked up the equipment, then spread conductive jelly over Annie's abdomen, and Rachel prayed as she had never prayed before. OK, so Annie had lost a lot of blood—too much, her professional instincts told her—but there was still a chance the baby might still be all right—there had to be.

'My baby's dead, isn't it?' Annie said, her voice devoid of all emotion as the technician swept the scanner over and over her stomach, desperately looking for signs of life. 'There's nothing there any more because my baby's dead.'

It was. Rachel kept on searching and searching the monitor well past the point when she knew it was hopeless, but eventually she knew she couldn't keep staring at it any longer. The baby had miscarried, and Annie and Gideon would have to be told.

Slowly she turned to face the couple, and hoped she would never have to see such heartbreak in two people's faces ever again.

'We've lost the baby?' Gideon said, clearly desperately

hoping she would contradict him, but she couldn't, and Annie broke down completely.

For a while Rachel let Gideon comfort his wife, but eventually she hesitantly touched him on the shoulder.

'Gideon, I'm sorry, but she has to go to Theatre. We need to…' She couldn't say the words. Couldn't say they had to perform a D and C—a dilatation and curettage—to remove the remains of the dead baby, but Gideon's jaw clenched nevertheless.

'I…I think Tom might still be on duty,' he said with difficulty. 'If he's not, we could page him at home…'

'I'll do the op,' Rachel said quickly. 'I'll phone Theatre and tell them we're on our way.'

The consultant tried to smile his thanks, and she hurried out to the phone, unable to bear the sight of his stricken face or to look at Annie any more lying so white and still on the consulting-room table.

The D and C wasn't a long operation. Once Annie's cervix was dilated it was a simple procedure to insert the curette into her uterus to remove the contents of her womb, but it was carried out in complete silence, and when it was over the anaesthetist and theatre staff followed Rachel into the changing room.

'Please, tell Gideon and Annie how sorry we are,' the anaesthetist said, his round, plump face showing his distress. 'I know words don't help, but…'

'And tell Mr Hart we're sorry, too,' the theatre sister said. 'He doesn't know yet, does he?'

Rachel shook her head. David was still operating in Theatre 2 with Barry and Sharon, and there hadn't seemed any point in pulling him out, not when there was nothing he could do, but he would have to be told. She just prayed it wouldn't be her who had to tell him.

'It's so unfair, isn't it?' the theatre sister continued huskily. 'Gideon and Annie… They're such a lovely couple, and for this to happen…'

'I know,' Rachel replied, and she did. Medically she

knew that as many as one in four pregnancies ended in a miscarriage. A defective embryo, the woman not producing enough of the right hormones, even fibroids could cause a miscarriage, but no amount of knowing it medically could have prepared her for it happening to Annie.

She wished she could cry. Perhaps if she could cry she would get rid of the cold, hard lump that seemed wedged in her throat, but she couldn't. All she could do was wait until the anaesthetist brought Annie round, then accompany her down to the ward in Obs and Gynae.

'You should go home,' Liz Baker said when she saw her. 'Gideon's sent for Tom, and we'll take care of Annie.'

They would, and yet still she lingered, all too heartbreakingly aware that there was nothing she could do, but wanting to be there in case Annie needed her.

'Look, you're not going to be much use to your patients tomorrow,' Gideon said eventually, 'and David's on his way up from the operating theatre.'

'Does he know what's happened?' she said, and the consultant nodded.

'I'm hoping he might be able to help. I've told Annie over and over again that it wasn't her fault, but I can't seem to get through to her.'

'Do you want me to talk to her?' she said quickly. 'We've become good friends—'

'Thanks, but I think the best thing you can do is go home.'

In other words, Annie didn't need her. She needed her husband and her brother, not somebody who was only a member of staff, and Rachel went home with an aching heart, and tried to forget, but she couldn't.

She switched on the television, only to switch it off again when the announcer said that the programme to follow was an in-depth, gritty documentary on the state of the National Health Service. She tried to read but, after staring at the first page of a book for more than half an hour, she tossed it aside.

Even when the thunderstorm Pam had predicted finally began, and she heard torrential rain bouncing in the street outside, she still couldn't erase the memory of Annie's devastated face and Gideon's pain-filled eyes.

Food, she told herself. Make yourself something to eat. OK, so you don't want to eat, but it will give you something to do. Wearily she went into the kitchen and took a can of soup from the cupboard, only to put it down again with a groan when she heard the shrill sound of her front doorbell.

Not Greg, she thought as she walked reluctantly down the hall to answer it. Please, don't let it be Greg, tonight of all nights. But it wasn't her cousin on her doorstep. It was David.

'I'm sorry—I shouldn't have come,' he said, as she stared at him, unable to disguise her surprise. 'It was a bad idea. I'll go…'

'You're soaking wet,' she exclaimed.

He looked down at himself blankly. 'Am I?'

'David, have you walked all the way here from the hospital?'

'I guess I must have,' he muttered. 'I don't remember. I'm sorry to have disturbed you—'

'For heaven's sake, come in,' she insisted. 'Come in, take off your jacket and I'll get you a towel.'

She ushered him into her sitting room, turned up the gas fire, though the night wasn't cold, and pulled a towel from the airing cupboard, but when she went back into the sitting room he was still standing exactly where she'd left him.

'Have you had anything to eat?' she asked, easing the sodden jacket from his shoulders.

'I…' He shook his head. 'I don't think so, but I'm not hungry.'

'Neither am I,' she said firmly, 'but we'll eat.'

They did. She heated up the can of soup, defrosted some rolls in the microwave and they ate, though she very much doubted whether either of them were aware of what they were eating. Both of them simply sat, wrapped in their own thoughts, and eventually Rachel said the words which were uppermost in her mind.

'How's Annie?'

David pushed his seat back from the table and stood up, his blue eyes dark and bitter. 'As well as can be expected. That's what we usually tell relatives, isn't it?'

'David—'

'Gideon says she'll probably be able to go home in a couple of days, but…' His jaw worked for a second, then he shook his head as though desperately trying to dispel the memories. 'Oh, hell, Rachel, it was awful. Annie was breaking her heart, and there was nothing I could do, nothing I could say. And Gideon… Did you see his face?'

'Yes,' she said with difficulty. 'Yes, I did.'

'I've never seen anybody look so desperate. I swear if I'd told him Annie would stop hurting if he cut off his right arm, he'd have done it.'

'He loves her, David,' she said softly, and he clenched his hands together until the knuckles showed white.

'Then I hope to God I never feel that way,' he exclaimed, and she felt a part of her heart wither and die. 'It's torn him apart, Rachel. Not just losing his child, but what it's done to Annie.'

'David—'

'Why did it have to happen? We're doctors, for heaven's sake. Things like this shouldn't happen to us, not with our experience.'

'I don't think experience has anything to do with it,' she murmured. 'When a woman miscarries it's usually because there's something wrong with the foetus—'

'It wasn't a bloody foetus,' he snapped. 'It was a *baby*. Annie and Gideon's *baby*.'

'I know,' she said, feeling the hard lump in her throat grow bigger and more painful. 'I know it was a baby, but I have to keep telling myself that it wasn't—not really—

not a properly formed baby—because if...' She tried to swallow, and couldn't. 'If I let myself think of it as a baby—Annie and Gideon's baby—then...'

She couldn't say any more, and he reached for her hand and grasped it tightly.

'Oh, hell, I'm sorry. Taking it out on you.'

'It's all right,' she managed to say. 'It's OK.'

'No, it's not. I'm always saying the wrong thing to you.'

'You're hurting, too—we all are.'

'I guess so. I...' He glanced at the clock on her mantelpiece. 'I'd better go. It's late, and you must be tired—wanting to go to bed.'

Rachel *was* tired. She did want to go to bed, but as he half turned her heart went out to him. He looked so lost, so drained that she said quickly. 'You don't have to go.'

His eyes met hers, uncertain and unsure. 'Rachel, are you saying...?'

'I'm saying I don't want to be alone tonight either,' she said. 'I don't want to think or to remember. I just want you to hold me, and be with me. And I think you need that, too.'

David didn't answer. He simply took her outstretched hand and she led him upstairs into her bed, knowing exactly what she was doing. That tonight would be the only night she would ever share with him, but it didn't matter. Tonight all she wanted was to hold him, to comfort him and to have him hold her. No strings, no talk of love or commitment, just to be with him and to forget.

He wanted that, too. She knew he did from the way he clung to her at first when their clothes were shed, burying his face deep in her neck so she couldn't see his tears, couldn't see him weeping for Annie and Gideon and the baby that would never be. She cried, too, feeling the hard cold lump in her throat ease, the pain in her heart lessen as she held him and stroked his back with her fingers and murmured over and over again, 'It's all right. I'm here. I'm here.'

He said very little, disjointed, half-formed phrases that she could barely hear and didn't understand. But it didn't matter. Nothing mattered tonight except their mutual need for one another, and it was a need. There was none of the passionate coupling that had been characteristic of their time together in York. None of the laughter or the mind-blowing heights he'd taken her to.

In its place there was an uncertainty about David that tore at Rachel's heart, a vulnerability that made her want to cry all over again. So that when he finally entered her, and whispered hoarsely, 'Rachel, forgive me,' she gave him all that she was, and could ever be, holding nothing back, asking nothing for herself in return, and took him deep within her to a warm and tender oblivion.

CHAPTER NINE

'YOU'RE early this morning, Mr Hart,' the porter commented as David strode through the swing doors of the Belfield Infirmary. 'Big day ahead?'

'Something like that,' David muttered, not halting his stride, but the porter wasn't discouraged and came after him.

'I was so sorry to hear about your sister, Doctor. Tragic, that's what it is. I was just saying to the wife this morning how tragic it was—ironic, too, what with your sister and Mr Caldwell both being doctors. Just goes to show you never know what's round the corner, doesn't it?'

David stepped into the lift and hit the button for the third floor. 'I'm sorry, but you'll have to excuse me…'

'I hear Dr Dunwoody was wonderful yesterday, taking control of everything. I have to say I've always thought her a bit of a cold fish myself, but—'

To David's relief the lift doors closed on whatever else the porter had been going to say, and he leant back against the wall and closed his eyes.

He supposed it was inevitable. People were bound to want to offer their sympathy, their condolences, and he was going to have to get used to it, but Rachel… Rachel was an entirely different matter.

Is that why you crept out of her house this morning like a thief in the night, his mind whispered, not even waiting for her to wake up?

He bit his lip savagely. He knew he should have stayed, but when he'd woken up and turned over to find her curled up beside him, her glorious auburn hair spread across the pillow, her lips slightly parted as though in a smile, he'd panicked.

Panicked because he'd known that when she woke up he'd have to talk about what had happened between them. Panicked because none of his usual glib 'Hey, wasn't last night great' phrases had seemed in any way suitable.

'You're very early, Mr Hart,' Pam said in surprise as he stepped out of the lift. 'Your first appointment's not until half past nine.'

'I know, but I've a pile of paperwork to catch up with,' he said quickly, hoping the flush of guilty heat he could feel creeping across his cheeks wasn't as visible as it felt. 'So I thought I'd come in early, make a start.'

Pam nodded her understanding. 'Would you like a coffee, Doctor?'

His empty stomach rumbled its agreement, and he nodded.

'Any cancellations today?' he asked as he accompanied her down the corridor, and she shook her head apologetically.

'I'm afraid it's wall-to-wall appointments again.' He wasn't surprised. It was never anything else. Pam continued, 'We're really going to miss Rachel when she goes back to Obs and Gynae, aren't we?'

'She's not leaving until her replacement has been appointed,' he replied, but that didn't seem to cheer up the receptionist.

'I know, but it won't be the same, will it? Not the same as having Rachel around. She was absolutely wonderful yesterday. I was dashing about like a headless chicken, but Rachel was terrific.'

He muttered something in reply—he didn't have the faintest idea what—and escaped with relief into his consulting room, but even that gave him no respite.

How could he have been so stupid? he wondered as he stared at the room's yellow walls and found himself remembering the hours he and Rachel had spent painting them. All his determination to back off, to treat her simply as a colleague, and yet still he'd ended up in bed with her.

Idiot. *Idiot.*

But you enjoyed it, didn't you? his mind whispered. You'd like to do it again.

Sure would, his body answered with unbridled enthusiasm, and he sat down at his desk with a groan. He never normally felt this way after good sex. Normally he felt terrific and full of energy, but today…

He felt depressed, and confused, because no matter which way he looked at it he knew that what he and Rachel had shared last night hadn't been just good sex. In fact, it had been like nothing he'd ever experienced before.

When he'd thought about making love to her before, he'd always assumed they'd rekindle the fire and passion they'd shared in York, but last night… Last night their love-making had been a tender, gentle comforting. A comforting that had reached down deep inside him, warming him, easing him, healing the cold aching pain in his heart, and it had been Rachel who had achieved the miracle. Rachel who had gathered him to her, held him, touched him, so that for the first time in his life it was the gentle touching and holding he remembered more than the physical act itself.

'Sorry to disturb you, Mr Hart,' Pam said as she opened his door, a cup of coffee in her hand, 'but Mr Caldwell's here.'

David was on his feet in an instant. 'Annie…?'

'She's fine, David,' his brother-in-law said quickly, appearing behind the receptionist. 'I just wanted a word.'

'Would you like a cup of coffee, Mr Caldwell?' the receptionist asked, as he pulled a seat over to David's desk, but he shook his head.

'Thanks, Pam, but I think I drank enough coffee last night to keep my caffeine levels well over the limit for weeks.'

'If there's anything else you want, just give me a shout, OK?' she said, and with a smile she withdrew.

'Nice woman,' Gideon observed as he sat down.

'You recommended well,' David replied, taking a gulp of his coffee, knowing the consultant hadn't dropped by to praise his receptionist but not wanting to push him into saying why he had come. 'How is Annie this morning?'

Gideon's jaw tightened. 'Tired, tearful. We're keeping her in for a few days, but...'

There was nothing more they could do—at least, not medically. David knew that, and Gideon did, too. Only time would heal, and even then not completely.

'I just wanted to thank you again for all your help last night,' Gideon continued. 'I really appreciate it.'

'She's my sister—you're my brother-in-law,' David said, not wanting to talk about last night but recognising Gideon's need to. 'I just wish I could have done more.'

Gideon rubbed his fingers over his unshaven cheeks, and sighed. 'Annie... She's talking about coming back to work after she's discharged.'

David's coffee slopped into his saucer as he sat up quickly. 'Is she out of her mind?'

'That's what I told her. I told her she needs time to grieve, to...'

Gideon shook his head, and David got to his feet and awkwardly put his arm round the consultant's shoulder. 'I'll talk to her.'

'I'd be grateful if you would. Maybe you can get her to see sense. I sure as hell can't.'

'It will come right, Gideon,' David murmured as he accompanied him to the door of the Mackenzie unit. 'I know it seems like the end of the world right now.' Lord, but was there ever such a trite observation? 'But it will come right.'

The consultant managed a wobbly smile but as he walked away, his shoulders hunched, his head down, David gritted his teeth until they hurt. He was a fine one

to talk about things coming right. How in the world was
he ever going to make things right between him and
Rachel?

If only he hadn't gone to her house. If only he'd simply
gone home. But somehow he'd found his feet walking towards Mount Stewart Street, and when she'd asked him to
stay…

'You remembered my cooking, huh?'

His heart sank as he recognised the all-too familiar
voice, and he turned reluctantly to see Rachel smiling at
him.

'Your cooking?' he said uncertainly, and her smile
deepened.

'I know you always said I couldn't boil water, but there
was no need for you to run off without having breakfast.
Even I can't ruin cereal or toast.'

Oh, hell, she looked so happy, and he had to puncture
that happiness. After last night she would be expecting
involvement, commitment from him, and he couldn't give
her either of those things, which meant she was going to
be hurt, and the last thing he'd ever intended had been to
hurt her.

'Rachel—'

'Do you want me to nip down to the canteen and get
you one of your disgusting salami and pickle and mayonnaise sandwiches?' she continued. 'You must be starv-
ing.'

'I'm fine. I'm…' Get it over with, he told himself. Tell
her that last night was a mistake. Tell her you're the biggest louse of all time, and get it over with. It will only
take a minute, and as long as she doesn't cry—please, God,
don't let her cry—it will be over with. 'Rachel, last
night—I never intended it to happen. I shouldn't have let
it happen, and I can only apologise.'

'Forget it.'

He blinked. *Forget it?* 'I know you said that you weren't
going to have any more flings, that you wanted commit-

ment, but I can't give you that, and you've every right to be angry with me, to feel that I perhaps used you…'

'Of course I don't feel used,' she protested. 'David, we both needed one another last night, so it's not a problem.'

Not a problem. What did she mean, it wasn't a problem? They'd made love, hadn't they? And all she could say was, 'Forget it. It's not a problem'?

Hey, don't knock it, a little voice warned in the back of his head. She's letting you off the hook, so quit while you're ahead.

But he didn't want to quit while he was ahead, not when she was standing there still smiling at him. He wanted to shake her.

'Rachel, you do understand what I'm saying?' he demanded. 'I know I said I wanted us to be lovers again, but I changed my mind, realised it was never going to work, so—'

'Last night was a one-off, and it didn't mean we were going to become involved again.' She nodded. 'I know.'

'You do?' he said faintly.

'David…' She put her hand on his arm, much as he imagined a teacher might do to a singularly dense pupil. 'Look, I know exactly why we made love last night. We were both feeling low, both in need of comfort, and it really isn't a problem.'

She meant it, he realised. She hadn't misunderstood him. She wasn't trying to wind him up, she actually meant it. A surge of anger flooded through him. Anger which was both stupid and irrational.

'Rachel—'

'Cripes, is that the time?' she said, glancing down at her watch. 'You'd better get a move on. Christine Grant will be here in five minutes for her check-up.'

She was leaving. She was actually walking away from him, and David said quickly, 'I'd like you to sit in with me.'

She looked surprised—he felt the same. 'Whatever for?'

she asked. 'You performed her fimbrioplasty, and she'll already have had her X-rays taken downstairs.'

'The follow-up will be good experience for you,' he said.

She stared at him silently for a second, and he wondered if she was going to point out—quite justifiably—that as she wasn't going to specialise in infertility treatment the experience would hardly be necessary, but she didn't. She simply shrugged in a whatever-you-say way and followed him into his consulting room, but there was no time to talk. Christine and her husband had arrived early and, efficient secretary that she was, Pam ushered them both in.

'I thought I'd have more energy by now,' Christine admitted when David asked how she was feeling. 'I mean, it's three weeks since my operation and yet I still feel pretty wiped out.'

'You had major surgery, Christine,' David said sympathetically, 'and we all take different amounts of time to recover from something like that. Now, let's take a look at your X-rays.'

Christine held out the envelope the X-ray department had given her, and David slipped the X-rays out, snapped them onto the screen and flicked on the light.

'It looks fine,' he murmured. 'What do you think, Dr Dunwoody?'

That 'fine' was the understatement of the year, she thought as she stared at Christine's Fallopian tubes. David had performed a fimbrioplasty, a technically difficult and very intricate operation to reconstruct the damaged fronded tissue at the end of one of Christine's Fallopian tubes, and yet now it was virtually impossible to distinguish between the fimbria that had been worked on and the one that had not.

'I think it looks amazing,' she said honestly, and Christine glanced from her to David, then back again.

'My operation's been a success, then?' she said, and Rachel smiled.

'I'd say so. Now all we can do is keep our fingers crossed that the tube catches and retains a fertilised egg.'

'Talking of fertilised eggs,' Mr Grant said awkwardly. 'When can Christine and I start making love again?'

'Whenever Christine feels physically comfortable enough to do it,' David replied, switching off the light over the X-ray screen, unsnapping the X-rays and putting them into Christine's folder. 'Is there a problem?' he continued, seeing the couple exchange glances.

'Not a problem as such, it's just…' Mr Grant crimsoned to the roots of his black hair, and his wife nodded her encouragement. 'Last week Christine and I were reading an article in a magazine that said it was vital for a woman to become pregnant as quickly as possible after tubal surgery. If she didn't then new adhesions would have a chance to form, and the surgery would have been pointless.'

David grinned. 'I'm afraid any adhesions that were going to form would have done so within twenty-four hours of Christine's operation, so unless you'd leapt on your wife as she was being wheeled out of the operating theatre, or while she was still in Recovery, you wouldn't have stood a chance of beating them.'

'But that means…'

'It means don't believe everything you read in magazine articles.' David laughed as Christine and her husband exchanged worried glances. 'So long as you didn't develop a tubal infection within the first few days of surgery—and, believe me, you didn't—there wouldn't be any adhesion development because the surfaces of your Fallopian tubes and uterus would have healed.'

Oh, but he was good, Rachel thought as the Grants smiled across at one another with clear relief. A top-of-the-range consultant, an excellent surgeon, and last night…

Last night had been wonderful, and despite his obvious thoughts to the contrary she had no regrets. She might have taken him to her bed because she loved him, but she hadn't expected anything back—certainly not commitment. Last night had been all about comfort and need, and she'd created a beautiful memory, a memory that would stay with her always.

'What are Christine's chances of becoming pregnant now she's had this operation?' Mr Grant asked as Christine rolled down the sleeve of her blouse after David had taken her blood pressure and pulse.

'Around forty-five per cent,' David replied, and Christine sighed.

'Not very good odds.'

'A lot better than the ones you had before,' David said encouragingly. 'And I'm not sending you away, saying, right, that's it, let's see what happens. I'll monitor you for a year, checking your ovulation levels every two months, and if you don't become pregnant I'll perform a laparoscopy to check out your Fallopian tubes and ovaries.'

'I thought she would have been more upbeat.' Rachel frowned when the Grants had left. 'Having had the operation, been given a very real possibility of becoming pregnant, I'd have thought she'd have been a lot more optimistic.'

'Women often become a bit down after tubal surgery,' David said as he put Christine's folder into his out-tray. 'Think about it, Rachel,' he said as she looked confused. 'Imagine for a second that I've just told you you're never going to have a child. How would you feel?'

She didn't have to imagine. She already knew. Knew that the baby she wanted was one that he and she would create, and it was never going to happen.

'Heartbroken,' she murmured. 'I'd be heartbroken that no child was ever going to call me Mummy. Heartbroken that I'd never be able to hold my own baby, watch its first steps, see it grow up.'

'OK, now fast forward a couple of years. How do you think you would feel about it now?'

'Resigned, I guess, but—'

'Right, now put yourself in Christine's shoes. Having been told you'll never have a baby, what if somebody like me came along, performed an operation and said now you have a possibility of having a child.'

'I see.' Rachel nodded. 'Before all I had was a definite no, and just as I was beginning to come to terms with that, you're now telling me there's a maybe.'

'Exactly.' He smiled. 'Sometimes a maybe can be infinitely harder to live with than a definite no.'

Not always, Rachel thought. When you and I were lovers in York, all I ever dreamt about were the possibilities. That one day you might fall in love with me. That I'd be the one woman you wouldn't walk away from. I'm older now—wiser—and I know that last night will never happen again, but right now, when you're smiling at me like that, it doesn't make it any easier to live with. It will in time— I know it will—but not right now.

She got to her feet. 'I'd better go. I have a full day ahead of me, and so do you.'

'Will you get a chance to go up and see Annie today?' he said as she walked to his door.

'I'm hoping so.'

'Me, too, And, Rachel…' She glanced over her shoulder at him, and he said awkwardly, 'Thanks for being so understanding about last night.'

'Hey, no problem,' she said lightly. 'And don't worry about Annie. It will get better. It might not seem that way at the moment but, believe me, it will get better.'

It didn't. In fact, as far as David was concerned, the next two weeks only succeeded in getting worse.

Rhona Scott came in for her appointment, and point-blank refused to listen to reason.

'She says she's going to pay for IVF treatment at a private clinic,' he fumed after the woman had gone. 'I told her that any clinic that agreed to put a woman with her medical history on a course of IVF was taking money under false pretences, but I may as well have talked to the wall.'

'I guess you just can't win them all, David,' Rachel said, but David didn't feel like he was winning any these days. Not when his sister returned to work just a week after she was discharged from Obs and Gynae.

'This is insanity, Annie,' he'd exclaimed when she'd stood in the middle of his consulting room, her face still far too white, dark shadows plain beneath her eyes. 'You should be at home, resting.'

'I would be at home if I'd been ill, David,' she said with a calmness that was infuriating, 'but I haven't. I've had a miscarriage. Lots of women have miscarriages, and they just get on with their lives.'

'But lots of women don't hold down a stressful, exhausting job in a hospital,' he protested. 'Annie, Gideon's worried about you—*I'm* worried about you—and if you'd just listen to me...'

'I will when you put your own life in order.'

'There's nothing wrong with my life,' he retorted without thinking, and saw his sister's eyebrows rise.

'Oh, really? So the fact you look as though you've lost a pound and found a penny means everything's all right, does it?'

'Don't start on me, Annie,' he warned, but she didn't listen.

'You want to know what I think, David?'

'No, but you're going to tell me anyway, aren't you?'

'I think you're in love with Rachel Dunwoody, but you're running scared of commitment, and I'm damned if I know why.'

He shut his desk drawer shut with a bang. 'That's the stupidest thing I've ever heard.'

'Don't call me stupid,' his sister exclaimed, and he gazed heavenward with exasperation.

'I didn't. I said what you just said was stupid, but if you keep this up...'

'Am I wrong?' his sister said, as he strode to his consulting-room door, and he rounded on her, keeping his temper with difficulty.

'Annie, why is it such a crime to like my life the way it is? Why can't you accept that I simply prefer all my relationships to be short and sweet?'

'I would accept it if I thought for one minute that you were happy, but you're not.'

'My sister, the amateur psychiatrist.'

'My brother, the commitment phobic,' Annie threw back at him before stomping away, leaving him glaring in frustration after her.

In love with Rachel Dunwoody? Of course he wasn't in love with Rachel Dunwoody. He wanted her. OK, all right, he was prepared to admit that he wanted her. Wanted to feel the gentle touch of her fingers on his body again, the warmth and softness of her skin beneath him, but that was just sex, and there was no way he was going to give up his comfortable, easygoing lifestyle just to enjoy some more good sex.

Which meant he kept a lid on his intrusive libido, and concentrated on his work, and his staff took to avoiding him as much as possible.

'I don't know what's got under Mr Hart's saddle recently,' Pam told Rachel, 'but I wish to heaven he'd get rid of it. Normally he's the most laid-back of men, but lately…'

'He's a complete pain in the butt,' Rachel finished for her ruefully. 'Tell me about it. We're interviewing for my replacement this morning so let's hope that puts a smile on his face for a change.'

It didn't. In fact, the interviews only resulted in making him even more irritable than ever.

'There's not one of them I'd employ for half a day, far less permanently,' he declared when the last of the interviewees had finally gone.

'Really?' Rachel said with surprise. 'I thought they were

all pretty impressive myself, and personally I'd be more than happy to work with Ian Gill.'

David sat back in his seat, his face tight. 'I'm not surprised, considering he seemed to spend the whole interview chatting you up.'

'He did not,' she protested. 'All he was doing was asking what I thought were very sensible questions about how the unit was run and—'

'He was chatting you up.'

'And you're being silly,' she said firmly. 'His qualifications and experience are far and away the best of those we saw.'

She was right, they were, but that didn't make David feel any more positively inclined towards Ian Gill. The man had been all over Rachel like a rash, and the thought of him working permanently at the Belfield, just two floors away from her...

'Judy Bolton wasn't bad,' he said.

'Not to mention also being very pretty,' Rachel said dryly, and he glanced across at her blankly.

'Was she?'

'Oh, come on, David, you're not asking me to believe you didn't notice. All that long blonde hair, and a figure half the male population of the Belfield would have wet dreams over?'

In truth, he hadn't noticed. All he'd been aware of had been that Dr Bolton had an annoying habit of flicking her blonde hair over her shoulder, and he'd found himself wondering why on earth she didn't do something sensible with it, like pinning it back into a neat French pleat.

'If you weren't keen on Judy Bolton, what about Margaret Simpson? Her references were excellent, and she's had three years' infertility experience.'

'Did you hear her laugh?' He shuddered. 'No, thanks.'

'What about Ben Thornton, then?' she suggested. 'I don't remember him laughing very much.'

'Probably because he also seemed barely able to string more than two words together,' he retorted, and she sighed.

'Look, David, what *do* you want in a specialist registrar?'

Somebody like you, he almost said, and just stopped himself in time because not even somebody like her would be any good. He wanted her. He wanted her to continue working with him, and she'd made it plain she didn't want to.

'Maybe the candidates we'll interview next week will be better,' he said, and saw her shake her head.

'They'd better be, David, because you're running out of time.'

Running out of everything, he thought as he left her consulting room. Running out of temper, and patience, and concentration, and it was all her fault.

Dammit, what was it about her that had got him so riled, and frustrated, and confused?

He'd tried telling himself she was no different to every other woman he'd made love to, but it hadn't worked. He'd tried telling himself that when she went back to Obs and Gynae he'd forget all about her in a week, but he knew it wasn't true. No one laughed the way Rachel did, nobody felt the way she did. They never had. She'd always been different, special.

Then maybe your sister's right? his heart whispered, and he sheered away from the thought quickly.

Of course Annie wasn't right. Commitment, marriage, a wife and a family? It wasn't for him. It might suit some men, but it wouldn't suit him, and if that made him selfish and arrogant, then so be it.

Rachel didn't think he was arrogant as she sat at her desk, lost in thought. She just wished he'd make up his mind. Hell, it should have been easy enough to have chosen one of the candidates they'd seen this morning. Every one of them had been far better qualified in infertility work than she was, and yet he hadn't liked any of them.

Her Aunt Mary would have said he was simply being thrawn—being difficult for the sake of being difficult—but it was more than that. For the past fortnight he'd been grumpy and irritable, and she would be glad when she was back in Obs and Gynae.

Except that she wouldn't be, not really.

Stop it, Rachel, she told herself firmly as she got to her feet and walked over to her filing cabinet. No regrets, remember? No looking back, only looking forward.

'Pam, do I have the application letters from the candidates Mr Hart will be interviewing next week?' she said as she heard her consulting-room door open behind her. 'Or does—?'

'Hello, Cousin Rachel.'

She straightened up slowly, feeling her heart leapfrog into her throat, and turned to see her cousin standing in the doorway. 'Greg… What…what are you doing here?'

'What else am I supposed to do when there's no other way I can contact you?' he demanded. 'If I call you at home I get diverted by the operator. If I call you at work some snippy receptionist tells me you're busy.'

'That's because I *am* busy, Greg,' she said. 'Look, maybe you could come round to the house one evening—'

'I'm sorry, Rachel,' Pam said breathlessly, appearing behind Greg, looking red-cheeked and dishevelled, as though she'd run down the corridor. 'He just walked straight past me. I told him you couldn't be disturbed, that he'd need to make an appointment…'

'It's all right, Pam.'

'Do you want me to call Security?' the receptionist continued, glaring up at Greg. 'Or I could get Mr Hart—'

'I said it's all right, Pam,' Rachel said firmly, and the receptionist glanced from her to Greg uncertainly.

'Are you sure?'

No, she wasn't sure, but admitting it wasn't going to help. 'I'm fine, Pam, honestly.'

The receptionist withdrew with obvious reluctance, and

Rachel took a steadying breath. 'I'm afraid I can only give you a few minutes, Greg.'

'Is the house sold yet?'

There was no point in lying to him. He'd only find out the truth eventually, and she shook her head. 'I keep telling you you've put too high a price on it.'

'Which is why I wanted to talk to you. I think we should lower the price.'

She gazed at him in amazement. 'Y-you do?'

'I've been thinking about what you said, and decided you're right. I want you to ring the estate agent and tell them to get whatever they can for the house.'

Something was wrong. All her instincts told her something was wrong. Greg was being sensible—too sensible—and it wasn't like him.

The words 'What are you up to?' sprang to her lips, and she crushed them down quickly. Did she really want to know? No, she didn't. All she wanted was him out of her life.

'You do realise that even if we lower the price, it might still take some time to find a buyer,' she said uncertainly, and he nodded.

'I understand. A lot of people don't want an old house. They want something modern, not something they're going to have to spend a lot of time and money on.'

He was smiling at her, and when he took a step forward she couldn't help herself. She backed up quickly, and saw his smile widen.

'What's wrong, Cousin Rachel? I thought this was what you wanted?'

It was, and yet…

'Everything all right in here, Dr Dunwoody?'

She groaned inwardly as David suddenly appeared in her doorway, his face tight, grim. Pam must have gone rushing off to get him, and she didn't want him here, didn't need him here.

'Everything's fine, Mr Hart,' she said. 'My cousin's just leaving.'

'Good,' David said, shooting Greg a glance that suggested if her cousin didn't leave pretty smartish he was shortly going to be helped on his way.

Greg looked David up and down. 'Who's this? Boyfriend or boss?'

'Mr Hart's my boss,' Rachel said quickly. 'Thanks for dropping by, Greg. I appreciate it, and I'll do what you said.'

'Do what?' David demanded the minute Greg had gone.

'He wants me to tell the estate agent to reduce the price of the house,' she replied, closing her filing cabinet.

'He's prepared to drop the price of the house?' he exclaimed. 'Rachel, I wouldn't trust that man as far as I could throw him. I think he's up to something.'

She did, too, but if reducing the price meant she'd get the house sold and Greg out of her life, she was more than happy to remain ignorant.

'I don't care what you think, David, and it's my problem, remember, not yours.'

'Of course it's my problem,' he exclaimed. 'That man's a criminal—you told me so yourself—and I'm worried about you.'

'Then you can stop worrying. As I've told you until I'm blue in the face, my private life is my own, and it's none of your business.'

'But, Rachel—'

'Read my lips, David. My problem. My life. My business. And now, if you'll excuse me...'

She didn't even give him the chance to reply. She simply strode past him and out into the corridor, and he went after her.

'Rachel, listen—'

'No, David, *you* listen,' she flared. 'I have managed to live my life quite satisfactorily without your interference for the last six years, and I fully intend to live the rest of

my life without your interference, too, so will you just...
just back off?'

And before he could stop her she strode away, leaving
him fuming in the centre of the corridor.

CHAPTER TEN

'I THOUGHT it would be Dr Dunwoody I'd see today. No
offence meant to you, of course, Mr Hart,' Sable Mitchell
added quickly, 'but I'm sure Dr Dunwoody said I would
be seeing her this morning.'

'I'm afraid Dr Dunwoody hasn't arrived for work yet,'
David replied. 'She had some private business to attend
to.'

Private business to do with selling her house, but that's
all I know, he thought grimly. Not that it bothers me that
I don't know anything else. Like hell it doesn't.

'Sable's been much better on the tamoxifen than she was
on the Clomid, Doctor,' Donald Mitchell said. 'She's not
been sick once, and there's been none of that constant
bleeding.'

'I'm very pleased to hear it,' David observed. 'How
about hot flushes?'

'Some, but they're not so bad I can't put up with them,'
Sable replied.

'Then I'll just check your blood pressure, pulse and
heart rate, and if they're fine, I'll make you an appointment
to see me again in another month.'

'Not Dr Dunwoody?' Sable queried, and David gritted
his teeth.

'I'm afraid Dr Dunwoody won't be working here next
month. She's primarily an Obstetrics and Gynaecology
doctor, you see, not an infertility expert,' he explained as
the Mitchells looked dismayed,' and she was only ever
working here temporarily. Next month she'll be returning
to her original post, and I'll have a new member of staff.'

Provided I can actually make up my mind as to who it's

to be, he thought glumly, because I didn't like the second batch of candidates any better than I did the first.

'I'm sorry to hear that,' Sable said. 'I really liked Dr Dunwoody, even if she isn't a proper infertility doctor. She was so kind when I had all that bother with the Clomid, and I'm going to miss her.'

So am I, David thought as he took Sable's blood pressure, then checked her pulse and heart. Rachel was an excellent specialist registrar, and her knowledge of infertility work was amazing considering it wasn't her speciality.

Oh, stuff her knowledge of infertility work, he thought savagely. I'm going to miss *her*. Miss her laughter, miss seeing her light grey eyes smiling up at me. Miss being able to see her every day, to hear her voice. Dammit, I'm even going to miss her irritating French pleat and her sensible work clothes.

'Is everything all right, Mr Hart?' Sable asked hesitantly, seeing a deep frown appear between his eyebrows.

'Fine—fine,' he said, forcing a smile to his lips. 'Your blood pressure, heart and pulse rate are completely normal, so we'll keep you on the tamoxifen and see how you get on.'

'Dr Dunwoody said we weren't to expect quick results,' Donald Mitchell said, 'but Sable and I were wondering…'

'How soon she might become pregnant?' David sighed. 'I'm afraid I can't answer that. Some women become pregnant within a few months of being on tamoxifen, but other women can take considerably longer. Three years isn't unusual.'

'Three *years*?' Sable said faintly, and David smiled sympathetically.

'I know it seems like a long time—and it is—but on the positive side, those women did eventually become pregnant.'

The Mitchells exchanged unhappy glances, but David knew he had to be honest with them. There was no point in suggesting the treatment would have instant results.

Sometimes it did, but the couple had to be prepared for the possibility of a very long wait.

'We'll see you in a month's time, then, Doctor,' Sable said as she and her husband got to their feet. 'And could you give my very best wishes to Dr Dunwoody? She's a lovely lady, isn't she?'

'Yes,' David muttered. 'Yes, she is.'

A lovely lady who was driving him crazy. Crazy because she was being so polite, so helpful and so unfailingly cheerful.

Of course he hadn't wanted her to tear his character to shreds every time she saw him. Neither did he want to see her looking sad and wistful because of what had happened on the night Annie had lost her baby. But when she'd told him to forget about what had happened, he hadn't expected her to so obviously completely forget about it herself.

Arrogance, a little voice at the back of his mind whispered. Just because you can't forget that night, you expect her to feel the same way, and you're angry because she doesn't.

No, not angry, he realised. Hurt.

As hurt as you felt when she left you in York with no forwarding address? his heart murmured, and he stamped on the thought immediately. The past was past, and it did no good to remember it. Especially when he had the depressing feeling that he was the only one remembering it.

He glanced at his watch. Coffee-time. Rachel, Annie and Pam would be having coffee in the staffroom. They'd be discussing patients, and appointments, and the frustration of not getting results back quickly enough from the lab, and that was what he needed. The boring hassle of everyday life in a hospital, not thinking about the past.

'Liz Baker and Sandy Fenton are getting *married*?' Pam exclaimed, spluttering over her coffee. 'Are you sure?'

'Liz told me herself when I met her in the lift this morning,' Rachel replied. 'Showed me her engagement ring, too, and it's lovely. An emerald and diamond cluster.'

'But they've only been dating…what, a little over a month?' the receptionist protested. 'Isn't it a bit soon to be thinking of marriage?'

'Sometimes it takes only one look to know you've met the man you want to spend the rest of your life with,' Annie said, helping herself to a chocolate biscuit.

'Yes, but *Sandy*?' Pam shook her head. 'I just hope she knows what she's doing.'

'I think it's romantic,' Rachel declared as she carried her empty coffee-cup over to the sink. 'OK, so Sandy might not be my idea of Mr Wonderful, but if Liz thinks he's the man for her, then I wish the two of them every happiness.'

'Wish who every happiness?' David asked as he strode into the staffroom.

'Liz Baker and Sandy Fenton,' Annie replied. 'They're getting married.'

'You're joking.'

'Nope, straight up, gospel truth. Liz told Rachel this morning,' Annie said, and a wave of bitterness surged through David.

Even Sandy Fenton could pull it off. Even boring, pedantic Sandy Fenton could win the girl of his dreams, and he couldn't even manage to persuade Rachel to continue working with him.

'I don't know who I feel sorriest for—Liz or Sandy,' he said more tartly than he'd intended, staring down into the biscuit tin. 'Hey, who's eaten all the macaroons?'

'You have,' his sister replied, 'and why should you feel sorry for Sandy or Liz? He might not be every woman's idea of the perfect man—'

'I meant them getting married,' he interrupted. 'What on earth do they need to get married for? It would be far more sensible if they simply lived together for a while, then when it doesn't work out, as it probably won't, they can go their separate ways with no hassle.'

Rachel rinsed out her mug and put it on the draining board with a bang. 'I suppose they want to get married because they're in love. People do fall in love, David,' she continued as he tried to interrupt. 'Even in the twenty-first century people still meet, fall in love and want to get married.'

'It still sounds stupid to me,' he muttered, and she nodded.

'Of course it does, because you haven't got a single romantic bone in your entire body, have you?'

'Rachel—'

'I'll see you later, Annie,' she said, deliberately cutting across him. 'I've Jennifer Norton in next for her monthly check-up, and I don't want to be late.'

'I'd better be going, too,' Pam declared, and as the two women walked out of the staffroom without a backward glance David turned to see his sister shaking her head at him.

'What?' he demanded. 'What have I done wrong now?'

'I want a DNA test,' she observed. 'I want a full, complete DNA test to prove you're actually my brother.'

'Of course I'm your brother.'

'Then how come you're so *stupid*?' she protested. 'Ever since you hit puberty you've always been able to charm any girl you've ever wanted out of her knickers, and to go and tell Rachel you don't believe in love…'

'Well, I don't,' he said, spooning some coffee into a mug. 'Not in the mushy until-death-us-do-part way you women do. Love is just a fancy name somebody dreamt up to describe a pretty basic physical act.'

'So you're saying that you don't love me or Jamie?'

'Of course I love you and Jamie,' he said irritably. 'You're my sister, he's my nephew, but the love Rachel was talking about… That's something completely different.'

His sister leant back in her seat, and folded her arms. 'How?'

'Because…because… Well, for a start I don't sleep with you or Jamie,' he retorted.

'You're talking about sex. I'm talking about love.'

'They're one and the same thing. Look, Annie, it's different for men,' he continued when she stared at him silently. 'You women like all the romantic hearts and flowers bit, but we men… We realise that what you call love is just something that's a whole lot of fun and satisfaction while you're doing it, but not something that's going to last.'

'So Gideon's going to up and leave me one day—that's what you're saying?'

'Of course he won't,' he exclaimed, appalled. 'Gideon and you—what you have is special.'

'And is what Helen and Tom have special too?'

'I don't know anything about their private lives—'

'And Sandy and Liz, and all the other married couples at the Belfield. They're all somehow special and unique, are they?'

She was twisting his words. David didn't know quite how she was managing to do it, but she was twisting his words.

'You don't understand, Annie.'

'Too damned right, I don't,' she retorted. 'All I know is Rachel is going back to Obs and Gynae soon, and I want to know what you're going to do about it.'

'Carry on with my work, of course,' he replied. 'Build this unit up until it's the best in Glasgow, push Admin to give me more facilities, maybe even my own operating team and lab—'

'And turn into a miserable, embittered old man while you're doing it,' she interrupted. 'David, how would you feel if Rachel left the Belfield?'

His eyes shot to hers. 'She's thinking of leaving the Belfield?'

'What's there here for her if she stays?' his sister countered. 'Her aunt's dead, her home's going to be sold and the only man she's interested in is my dumb brother who's in love with her.'

'I'm not in love with her.'

'Who's in love with her,' she emphasised, 'and yet for some crazy reason known only to himself refuses to commit. Would you want to stay on here if you were her?'

David stared at his sister with dismay. Rachel wouldn't leave. She couldn't. If she left...

His life would be empty again as it had been for the last six years. Empty, and shallow, and worth nothing.

Annie was right. He was in love with Rachel. He'd fallen in love with her at the Hebden, but before he'd been able to tell her how he felt she'd gone, leaving no forwarding address. Gone because she hadn't loved him.

He could still remember the day her landlady had told him she'd moved to London. It had been as though somebody had plunged a knife into his heart, then twisted it, and it had been then that he'd started running away from relationships. Running because he never, ever wanted to feel that depth of pain again.

'David...?'

His sister's face was troubled, worried. He tried to smile, but failed miserably.

'You don't understand, Annie,' he murmured, and she came over to him and clasped her hands in his.

'Then *tell* me,' she said. '*Tell* me, so I do understand.'

'Love doesn't last—not for me. Some people—people like you and Gideon—are lucky. They meet, fall in love and it lasts, but it doesn't last for me.'

The faint markings of a frown appeared on her forehead. 'When did you decide that it wouldn't last for you?'

He pulled his hands out of hers impatiently. 'Does it matter?'

'There was somebody once, wasn't there?' she said softly. 'Somebody you loved, but she left you, and that's why you believe that love doesn't last. Was...was it Rachel?'

'No, it wasn't,' he lied, but his sister knew he was lying.

'Oh, David, why have you made such a damn mess of everything?' she exclaimed. 'Why have you done nothing but try to flirt with her ever since you met her again, making her think all you wanted was her back in your bed for another brief fling?'

He didn't know. Yes, he did. Self-preservation. He might not have realised it at the time, but he'd deliberately gone out of his way to make Rachel think his feelings were purely physical to protect himself if it all went wrong again.

'David, it's not too late,' Annie said, scanning his face anxiously. 'She loves you. I know she does,' she insisted as he shook his head. 'Tell her how you feel. Tell her you love her.'

Could he? He forced himself to think back to the night when he and Rachel had made love, how she'd asked nothing for herself, seeming only to want to help him, to comfort him. Maybe she did love him, but to ask her if she did, to risk rejection... He couldn't do it.

'It's no use,' he muttered, and his sister shook her head with exasperation.

'Of course it is. David—'

'Annie, it's no use,' he flared. 'Rachel's going back to Obs and Gynae, and I'm getting on with my life. End of story.'

And it was the end of the story, he told himself as his sister sighed and walked slowly out of the staffroom. Rachel didn't care for him now any more than she had in York, and there was no way he was going to put his heart on the line again. No way.

'Your blood pressure's pretty good this morning.' Rachel smiled as she unwrapped the cuff from Jennifer's arm. 'I'll just take your pulse, weight you and then it's time for—'

'Another scan.' Jennifer sighed. 'It always seems to be time for another scan.'

'At least you won't be having too many more now,' Rachel said bracingly. 'Actually, just another two—you're thirty-one weeks pregnant. Just two more scans, and two more injections of magnesium sulphate, and then it will be show time.'

'I wish it was show time now,' Jennifer said, shifting uncomfortably in her seat. 'I feel like a beached whale.'

'It's because you're carrying twins. Two babies always mean a greater weight gain, and I'm afraid the pre-eclampsia adds even more.' Jennifer didn't reply, and Rachel squinted at her thoughtfully. 'You OK?'

'I'm a bit iffy this morning, actually. Brian did the cooking last night, and I'm wondering if perhaps he didn't cook the meat thoroughly.'

'Tummy cramps?'

'Not exactly cramps, more twinges. It's nothing to worry about, Doctor,' Jennifer continued as Rachel's eyes narrowed.

'Nevertheless, I think I'll take a quick look at you,' Rachel said. 'If you could get up onto the examination—'

She didn't get any further. Jennifer suddenly doubled up with a sharp cry of pain, and to Rachel's dismay a gush of clear fluid flooded down the woman's legs onto the consulting-room floor. It hadn't been Brian's cooking that was making his wife feel queasy. She was in labour.

With a muttered oath Rachel hit her intercom button. 'Pam, tell Mr Hart I need him here right away, then phone the intensive baby care unit and Maternity, and tell them I need them, too. Jennifer Norton's in labour.'

'She's *what*?' Pam squeaked. 'But, Rachel—'

'Just *do it*, Pam.'

The intercom went dead, and Rachel turned back to Jennifer with what she hoped was her most calming, encouraging smile.

'Hey, look on the bright side. At least you won't need

to have any more scans or injections of magnesium sulphate.'

'But it's too soon, Doctor, far too soon,' Jennifer cried. 'They're not due for another nine weeks.'

'Babies have survived at twenty-eight weeks—even at twenty-four,' Rachel declared, helping Jennifer up onto the examination table and trying hard not to remember what had happened in this very room to Annie's baby.

'But Brian... He's supposed to be my birth partner—and he's going to be so disappointed,' Jennifer exclaimed, then let out a loud shriek as a contraction hit her.

Brian Norton's disappointment is the least of my worries, Rachel thought grimly, snapping on a pair of surgical gloves and easing Jennifer's panties down. Jennifer's cervix had already dilated to ten centimetres, and if the team from ICBU didn't arrive soon, the babies would be there before they were.

But not before David. She heard the sound of running feet in the corridor outside, then her consulting-room door banged open and he was at her side.

'Going for experience in maternity work now, are you?' He grinned.

'Not willingly, I can assure you,' she replied. 'Cervix dilated to ten centimetres, contractions coming every three minutes.'

'The ICBU team?'

'On its way.' Jennifer let out another shriek, and Rachel winced. 'At least, I hope they are.'

'You're doing fine, Jennifer,' David declared, catching hold of the woman's hand. 'Just keep on pushing and panting the way you're doing, and everything will be just fine. Rachel, have you a cushion?'

A cushion. She stared at him blankly. What did he need a cushion for? They didn't need a cushion, they needed the ICBU team. They weren't maternity experts—she wasn't a maternity expert. What if Jennifer needed an urgent blood transfusion? What if one of the babies was a breech or had the cord tangled round its neck? It could all go wrong as it had gone so horribly wrong for Annie, and she didn't want that responsibility. Not again.

'Rachel.' She stared at David in panic, and he said softly, 'This isn't Annie, Rachel. Now, have you got a cushion?'

'Yes—yes, I have,' she said jerkily, and opened her cupboard and pulled one out.

'One of the babies' heads is crowning,' he exclaimed, taking the cushion from her and slipping it beneath Jennifer's head. 'Relax, Jennifer, relax, and work with the pain, not against it.'

'Oh, damn, blast and sugar, that's easy for you to say,' she huffed, throwing him a look that would have killed.

Rachel gave a hiccuping laugh. 'That's my girl, Jennifer. You tell him.'

'Baby number one coming,' David cried, and he was right.

With a rush and a slither, the tiny scrap of humanity suddenly slipped out into his hands just as Rachel's consulting-room door opened for a second time and a sea of smiling faces appeared.

'Somebody call for the ICBU team?'

'Cutting it a bit fine, aren't you?' David replied, holding the baby out to them.

'Hey, we like to give you ordinary working consultants a bit of practice occasionally,' the sister from ICBU announced. 'One lovely baby boy. Any more on the way, or is that it?'

'Push, Jennifer, push,' Rachel said as the woman let out a cry that was almost a sob. 'Your son's waiting for his sister.'

'And bang goes the surprise element.' David grinned as Jennifer bore down heavily, her face scarlet. 'Sorry about that, Jennifer, but I'm afraid Dr Dunwoody's a bit of a blabbermouth.'

'I...I don't care,' Jennifer gasped. 'I just... Oh, cripes, it hurts, it hurts.'

'Not for much longer, I promise,' he said encouragingly. 'Just give me one more push—a really big one this time. Good...good... Your daughter's almost here. Keep pushing, keep pushing... Excellent!'

Better than excellent, Rachel thought as the baby slid, protesting, into the world. They were here. Jennifer's babies were both here and, though they were tiny, she'd seen far smaller babies survive under the care of the ICBU team.

'Congratulations, David,' she said when Jennifer's twins had been whisked away and the maternity team had taken charge of their mother.

'Hey, it was a three-person team effort,' he protested. 'You, me and Jennifer.'

'More you and Jennifer than me,' she said ruefully, and he shook his head.

'It was a three-person team effort. And we do make a good team.' He took a deep breath. 'And talking of teams—'

'I was just wondering if I should phone Jennifer's husband—tell him what's happening?' Pam interrupted. She glanced round the consulting room and let out a low whistle. 'Cripes, but it looks as though you need some cleaners in here.'

'It does a bit, but it was all in a good cause.' Rachel smiled, and the smile tugged at David's heart, urging him onwards.

'I meant what I said about us making a good team,' he said the moment the receptionist had gone with instructions to phone Brian Norton. 'Rachel, it's not too late for you to change your mind about going back to Obs and Gynae. In fact, I'd very much like for you to change your mind and stay on in the unit as my specialist registrar.'

'You would?' she said with an expression he didn't understand.

'As I told you before, you have a real talent for this work and…well, the people I've interviewed,' he floundered, completely unnerved by her steady gaze, 'I don't know them, but I know you, and it would be so much easier for me if I could continue working with you.'

'Easier,' she repeated.

'I know it's been exhausting with just you, me and Annie,' he continued doggedly, 'but once we're fully staffed it will be different, and—'

'David, I'm very flattered,' she interrupted, 'but I like my work in Obs and Gynae. It's where I belong.'

He stared at her silently for a second, then nodded. 'I see.'

'And speaking of where I belong,' she continued, 'is it all right if I leave the unit for about an hour? There's some people who would like to see round the house, and it's the only time they can come, and it is my lunch-hour—'

'Fine,' he said with an effort. 'Just try not to be back too late. We've a packed afternoon ahead of us.'

'Right, and thank you, that's terrific,' she said with obvious relief, but he didn't feel relieved, and he felt even worse when he walked out of Rachel's consulting room and straight into his sister.

'Is that the best you can do—wittering on about how much easier it would be to work with her rather than somebody else?' she hissed, but he pushed past her, not wanting to hear.

Three weeks. He still had three weeks left before Rachel went back to Obs and Gynae, and during that time he was bound to find the right moment, the right opening, to say what he wanted. It was all a question of timing.

More a question of courage, his heart whispered, and he sighed inwardly. Would he ever have the courage to say right out, 'Rachel, I love you?'

He doubted it. He hoped he could, but he'd feel like such a fool if she turned him down flat. Exactly as she'd turned him down flat in York by taking off without a word of farewell.

Enough, he told himself angrily. Enough of this. Go, get some lunch, but not your usual sandwiches in the staff-room where Annie will collar you. Take yourself off to the canteen for some peace and quiet.

There wasn't much peace to be had in the canteen, not with it packed to the walls with chattering doctors, nurses and lab staff, but at least none of them were talking to him, and he didn't have to defend himself or his actions.

'Not often we see you down here, Mr Hart,' Liz said as he passed her on the way out.

'Too busy normally, Liz,' he replied, then paused. 'I heard about your engagement. Congratulations.'

'Why, thank you.' She smiled. 'I know Sandy and I have been the butt of quite a few hospital jokes since we announced it, but we love each other, and that's the most important thing, isn't it?'

'Sure is.' He nodded, and on impulse he bent down and kissed her cheek. 'I hope you're very, very happy.' And before the stunned sister could say anything, he smiled and walked quickly away, so quickly that he almost collided into one of the hospital paramedics who was running to-wards the ambulance bay. 'Hey, where's the fire?' he pro-tested.

'Not funny, Doc,' the paramedic replied. 'That's exactly where we're headed. Big fire in Mount Stewart Street— one casualty so far.'

'Mount Stewart Street?' David repeated, feeling his heart clutch in his chest. 'What number in Mount Stewart Street?'

'Number 53,' the paramedic threw over his shoulder as he raced on.

Rachel's house, and she'd gone there in her lunch-hour to show some people round. Oh, dear God, *no*. Not Rachel. If he should lose her now…

Without even thinking about it, he broke into a run. 'Wait—I'm coming with you.'

'But you're not an A and E medic, Doc,' the paramedic protested, clearly startled.

'A member of my staff lives there,' David replied. 'Rachel Dunwoody.'

'Yes, but…' The paramedic took one look at David's face, and clearly decided against further argument. 'Fine, Doc, whatever you say.'

It was the longest journey of David's life. The ambulance travelled at breakneck speed, going through red lights, mounting the pavements at times to get past the traffic, but still it seemed to take a lifetime to get to Mount Stewart Street. But when they arrived it wasn't relief David felt but horror.

The paramedic had said there was a big fire. What he hadn't said was that the house was completely ablaze, and nobody inside could possibly have walked away unharmed.

'Dear lord,' David whispered as he stepped out of the ambulance, and the heat of the flames almost took his breath away. 'Rachel. Oh, my God, *Rachel*!'

'You're getting in the way here, mate,' a burly fireman declared, dragging a hose forward to join the others that were already playing on the burning building.

David grasped hold of his arm quickly. 'The casualty—where's the casualty?'

The fireman jerked his head to one side. 'Over there with the police, and I know what I'd like to do with him.'

Him? It was a *man* who had been injured, not Rachel? Then where—?

'David, what on earth are you doing here?'

He whirled round to see a pair of familiar clear grey eyes staring up at him, and knew that he'd just been given all his Christmases and birthdays in one.

'Rachel, you're all right,' he gasped. 'You're *all right*!'

'Of course I am,' she protested as he pulled her into his

arms and hugged her, knowing he never wanted to let her go. 'The house was on fire when I got here. Bit of a problem as the people I was supposed to be showing it to arrived at the same moment. Needless to say, they're not putting in an offer.'

He laughed shakily into her hair. 'But the casualty—who's the casualty?'

'Greg. Remember how he told me that it didn't matter what I got for the house? Well, he'd clearly worked out that if he burned it down he'd get a whole lot more money on the insurance. Unfortunately he put his foot through one of the rotten floorboards in the vestibule as he was leaving and broke his leg, and that's where the police and firemen found him.'

'Not what you'd call a very successful arsonist,' David observed, trying and failing to stop a grin from spreading across his face, and Rachel's lips curved.

'Well, he managed to burn down the house, but I see what you mean.' A loud crash suddenly echoed behind them, and as she glanced over her shoulder, the amusement faded from her face. 'It's all gone, David. My home, all my mementoes of my aunt and my parents, it's all gone.'

He hugged her tighter. 'I'm sorry—so sorry.'

Tears sparkled in her eyes, and she dashed her hand across them quickly. 'I know you are, but right now… Right now, it doesn't help.'

'Oh, Rachel—'

'Sorry to interrupt, love, but could you give us an address where we can contact you?' a policeman said as he joined them, and Rachel eased herself out of David's arms.

'I don't know,' she said uncertainly. 'I'll probably be staying in a hotel or bed and breakfast. Look, can I phone you later when I'm settled?'

The policeman nodded but when he walked away David caught hold of her by the shoulders and said determinedly, 'You are not—repeat *not*—moving into a hotel or a bed and breakfast.'

'But it will be perfect,' she replied, clearly striving to be brave, which only tore at his heart more. 'All my meals laid on, my room cleaned every day, my bed made. What more could a girl want?'

'A hotel is not a home,' he said. 'You can stay with me.'

'I couldn't possibly impose—it wouldn't be right.'

'Who's imposing?' he demanded impatiently. 'And why wouldn't it be right? Rachel, I'm not inviting you into my home so I can make love to you morning, noon and night. I have a perfectly respectable spare bedroom. Annie used it when she stayed with me.'

'You don't understand,' she replied. 'I don't know how long it's going to take to find somewhere to live. I've got no money except my salary. The only clothes I have left are those I'm wearing. It could be months before the insurance on the house is settled, and maybe not even then because it was arson.'

'Then stay with me for months.' David took a deep breath. 'Stay with me for ever if you want.'

She laughed a little shakily. 'Wouldn't that rather cramp your style with your future girlfriends?'

'There aren't going to be any future girlfriends, Rachel. I only want one woman in my life, and that's you.'

She stared up at him open-mouthed, then shook her head. 'You're just saying that because you feel sorry for me, and I appreciate it, but—'

'I do *not* feel sorry for you,' he exclaimed. 'Rachel, I *love* you, and I want to marry you.'

'But—'

'Rachel, there have been many other women in my life, but none of them have ever been in my heart. You—only you—have ever been there. I know I messed things up before. I know I'm a jerk. The only sensible thing I've ever done in my life was to fall in love with you, and I want you to make my heart your home.'

Her face crumpled. 'Oh, David, you can't be in love with me.'

'That's what I've been trying to tell myself for the last six years,' he said huskily, 'but it hasn't worked. I would have told you how I felt before in York, but you ran away.'

'I ran because I thought *you* didn't love *me*,' she protested, and he gathered her to him with an uneven chuckle, and said, 'We're a prime pair of idiots, aren't we?'

'Speak for yourself,' she said into his chest, and he laughed and held her tighter.

'So, will you come home with me and marry me as soon as possible?' he murmured, kissing her hair, her forehead.

'Maybe we should just live together, then if it doesn't work out, we can walk away with no hassle,' she observed. 'That's what you said Liz and Sandy ought to do.'

'Which only goes to prove that I *am* an idiot,' he exclaimed. 'We're getting married, Rachel.'

She sighed into his neck. 'Bossy, aren't you?'

'Is that a yes?'

She looked up at him, her eyes shining with love, and laughter, and some unshed tears. 'That's a yes, David.'

He kissed her long and hard and deep, and when she surfaced breathlessly, he smiled down at her, his blue eyes glinting. 'There's just one thing, Rachel.'

'One thing?' she echoed.

'I don't suppose there's any chance in the near future of you hiring that Nell Gwynn costume again—purely for a private viewing this time.'

Her lips twitched. 'Only if you hire out the Dick Turpin one, too.'

'Got a thing about highwaymen, have you?' he said, his voice a soft whisper of laughter.

'Not highwaymen, no. Regency costumes. I've always found them…rather sexy.'

'Sexy, huh?' He grinned. 'Well, I happen to think Restoration costumes are sexier.'

'You could be right,' she said thoughtfully, 'because I

read in a book that women of that time didn't actually wear any underwear. None at all.'

'Is that right?' he said, his voice suddenly husky.

'Uh-huh.'

'So if we stopped by Kendra's on our way home this evening, and you managed to hire that costume again, and you put it on for me tonight…'

'That would be for me to know, David, and you to find out.' She chuckled, and he laughed, too, and gathered her into his arms and kissed her.

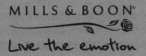

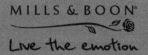

MILLS & BOON

BETTY NEELS

THE CHRISTMAS COLLECTION

On sale 5th December 2003

Available at most branches of WH Smith, Tesco, Martins, Borders, Eason, Sainsbury's and all good paperback bookshops.

FREE!

4 Books
and a surprise gift!

We would like to take this opportunity to thank you for reading this Mills & Boon® book by offering you the chance to take FOUR more specially selected titles from the Medical Romance™ series absolutely FREE! We're also making this offer to introduce you to the benefits of the Reader Service™—

★ FREE home delivery
★ FREE gifts and competitions
★ FREE monthly Newsletter
★ Books available before they're in the shops
★ Exclusive Reader Service discount

Accepting these FREE books and gift places you under no obligation to buy; you may cancel at any time, even after receiving your free shipment. Simply complete your details below and return the entire page to the address below. *You don't even need a stamp!*

YES! Please send me 4 free Medical Romance books and a surprise gift. I understand that unless you hear from me, I will receive 6 superb new titles every month for just £2.60 each, postage and packing free. I am under no obligation to purchase any books and may cancel my subscription at any time. The free books and gift will be mine to keep in any case.

M3ZEF

Ms/Mrs/Miss/Mr ....Initials...............................
BLOCK CAPITALS PLEASE

Surname..

Address..

....

....Postcode ....

Send this whole page to:
UK: The Reader Service, FREEPOST CN81, Croydon, CR9 3WZ
EIRE: The Reader Service, PO Box 4546, Kilcock, County Kildare (stamp required)

Offer not valid to current Reader Service subscribers to this series. We reserve the right to refuse an application and applicants must be aged 18 years or over. Only one application per household. Terms and prices subject to change without notice. Offer expires 27th February 2004. As a result of this application, you may receive offers from Harlequin Mills & Boon and other carefully selected companies. If you would prefer not to share in this opportunity please write to The Data Manager at the address above.

Mills & Boon® is a registered trademark owned by Harlequin Mills & Boon Limited.
Medical Romance™ is being used as a trademark.